THE GILDED ONES

THE GILDED ONES

BROOKE FIELDHOUSE

Matador
9 Priory Business Park,
Wistow Road, Kibworth Beauchamp,
Leicestershire. LE8 0RX
Tel: 0116 279 2299
Email: books@troubador.co.uk
Web: www.troubador.co.uk/matador
Twitter: @matadorbooks

ISBN 978 1789013 993

British Library Cataloguing in Publication Data.
A catalogue record for this book is available from the British Library.

Printed and bound in Great Britain by 4edge Limited
Typeset in 11pt Adobe Garamond Pro by Troubador Publishing Ltd, Leicester, UK

Matador is an imprint of Troubador Publishing Ltd

Fred & Fanny, for the title.

'Lord, what fools these mortals be!'
A Midsummer Night's Dream, William Shakespeare

PROLOGUE

The car in front is a Porsche Targa 911, colour red. I'm not sure what I'm driving.

I'm alone in my vehicle but I can see two heads in the Targa. The driver; bobbed hair, female – definitely female, I can see that as she turns to the right to speak to her passenger. Her mouth doesn't move because he – if it *is* a he – is doing the talking. I can't be sure… but I think she's smiling. Her lips part, nose upturns, tiny chin tilts.

Her profile vanishes and his appears – yes definitely a '*his*'; rounded chin, overbite and pout to top lip; a beaky nose. The sun in front of us is strong and it's like watching a pair of Edwardian seaside silhouettes which have come to life.

We're climbing, and it feels like morning. The road is clear and wet, but everywhere else is coated with snow; a solid wall of it on my right, and to the left a rampart of white. She's driving fast and I'm doing well to keep up, but I have a strange feeling that I'm late for something.

Every time we pass under a bridge there's a whooshing from above, a drumming from below, and the sucking of rubber on tarmac. Ahead the road appears to be blocked by towering rock, but into a tunnel we shoot, swallowed by pouting lips of polished concrete. Whoosh becomes hiss. The drumming turns from paradiddle to tom-tom, and I can see the two heads in front of me high-keyed by the sodium lights on the sides of the tunnel.

For a few magical moments it's as if the Edwardian silhouettes have been endowed with extra life in the form of a third dimension. I can see that her bob is brunette, can pick out the pin-pricking of his close-cropped sandy hair, and as our cars flash past the lights I can see flesh shining on foreheads, and on cheeks. Then out we pop, back into limitless Alpine space, and once again the heads return to the two-dimensional world of chattering black paper cut-outs.

I can see distant mountains, scree coated with blanched scrub, cuckoo-clock houses piled formlessly on the slopes. We bend to the right, left, right again. The same cuckoo clocks appear first on one side, then on the other as we climb the slalom. How clever I seem to be at keeping a constant distance from the Targa! It's as if I'm being pulled along, but as we descend I'm getting nearer and in the valley bottom, the Targa stops in a scrubbed conurbation of cuckoo clocks. The sun is on our left and I can see her eyes in the rear mirror. They're a lovely pale blue. I can watch her reading the signpost and I know that if she turns left or right I will lose her for ever. But on she goes, straight on.

We're climbing again and the Targa is pulling away from me. I can see his hand waving between the two seats, see her eyes scintillating as she accelerates up into the mountains. Another whoosh as we go under a bridge and the road turns sharply to the left. The bend seems to go on for ever and when the road straightens up, the car in front has vanished. I know it's gone because I can see the road for miles ahead.

I stop my car, reverse into a lay-by and before I even pull on the handbrake I can see what's happened. Instead of a steel barrier at the roadside there's a line of small white-painted concrete bollards. Two are missing.

I open my door and how cold the air outside is! It's as if I've awakened from sleep and I notice I'm wearing little more than chinos and a cheesecloth shirt. I bang the door, pad across asphalt onto snow-covered scree. I can't see over the edge so I need to shuffle further down the slope to get a view of what's happened.

I look up the road, and back across an expanse of white towards the last bridge. There's nobody. There's been nobody the whole time I've been following the Targa, and I can feel that chill of the spleen, the tingling of the buttocks, and I know I must push myself just that bit further so I can look over the edge.

I hear the chock of the scree as I wade down... feel the squeak of tightly packed snow. Once or twice I'm forced to bend, and my fingers touch the cold wetness, but it doesn't seem to hurt. I notice – quite ridiculously – that I'm wearing nothing on my feet other than beige espadrilles.

When I see the missing car, I'm surprised it's still facing the way we were travelling. It's upside down and its dark bronze underbelly is full of black geometric crevices. It looks longer than it did when it was on the road and it casts a blue shadow across the bed of snow where it's come to rest.

There's a figure standing by the driver's door, a splash of colour; head and shoulders visible in the sunlight... No sign of the man but there's no smoke, no fire, and had there been no evidence of life I would have driven back to the village for help. What I'm going to do is climb down and comfort the lady. If the man is alive then perhaps I can help him too.

The descent takes much longer than I thought. Every so often I stop to get my breath and to listen for traffic on the road above, but there isn't any. Down here everything seems much bigger than it did from the lay-by. What looked like moss or scrub with a drizzle of ice crystals are really fifty-foot-high trees, and there are ravines you could get lost in. I'm not sure that I'll be able to get back.

Perhaps when I reach the crash site there will be a first-aid kit, bottled water, blankets, maybe even a picnic basket. I keep losing sight of the car and every so often I hear the gentle susurrations of a partly frozen stream. My espadrilles are soaking.

At last I'm standing looking at the passenger side of the car and I'm sorry to have to report that the man is dead. There's a narrow trail of blood beneath the beaky nose – except now it's above the beaky nose because everything is upside down. I know he's dead because being inverted is clearly of no discomfort to him. No sagging jowls, no swollen eyes, or purple ears. Gravity is no longer of importance to this body and for the first time I see him as a fully three-dimensional presence. There's sunlight modelling his chin, and the dome-like head with its millimetre-long sandy hair. He reminds me of a giant foetus suspended in liquid, and most definitely one in a jar, not in the womb. Thank God, *she's* alive.

There's no sound, only that hiss, the one which quantum physicists claim is the fizz after the Big Bang. The engine must be switched off and she's standing by the open driver's door, motionless, her bobbed hair immaculate. The air is still and there's a feeling of perfection as if I'm looking at an advert for motoring in Switzerland – except the car happens to be upside down. The sooner I get to her the better.

'Are you all right?'

Her reply puzzles me.

'I'm Freia... It's spelled the German way.'

The voice is not what I'd expected. It's deep and seems to rise from the valley bottom. I catch sight of her cotton top, pink with white Aztec pattern.

'Hold on, I'm coming.'

I pull myself across to her side, my hands resting on the underneath of the car, dark metal warmed by sun and recent internal combustion. She's wearing skinny scarlet jeans, and the mountains behind her look like fresh oyster shells stacked on some vast fishmonger's stall.

On her feet are shiny mink-hued ballet pumps, *en pointe*. I stare at the tips of the pumps and cover my mouth with both my hands. My spleen drops past zero, through the valley bottom and into the void. I look at her eyes, no longer scintillating as they did when she read the signpost. The figure is suspended invisibly and diabolically, one foot above the snow-covered ground.

ONE

The head in front of me was resting. Tilted back on the train seat headrest, ears plugged with pearl-like speakers, eyes closed, hands at prayer. Between the palms was a silver Walkman.

The young man looked like how I wanted to be. Last night's dream had zapped me. What I needed was at least a morning to recover, and here I was on the 0730hrs on my way to a job interview. That's the way it is these days, you don't wait for promotion, or to get headhunted. You play the field, you move on.

It was time I did. I had to get away from Geoff.

'Pulse… What you need is a nice young lady. You're what… thirty-five? How can you be so selfish still living on your own? There's no substitute for family life.'

Mrs Geoff was pregnant and there was a two-year old. After these 'lectures' I was often forced to stand and watch him flirt with the prettier girls on my design team, and later that year, after he and my team leader Ros had been on a business trip which involved a hotel stay, she came to speak to me.

'Pulse, you know I'm more than capable of taking care of myself but can we do anything about that arsehole?'

I advised her not to rock the boat by taking the subject any further.

I looked again at the boy opposite... a bit more than half my age. His hair was fashionably short at the back and sides and billowing at the front like an amber plume of smoke. The traces of henna reminded me of my own hair experiments of not long ago.

'Is Pulse there?' a client had asked.

'Ye-es, he's inside,' replied a colleague.

'Ooooh, all those mirrors... he's probably checking his hair colour!'

I decided it was high time to call time on that little experiment.

The boy opposite me opened his eyes... Seemed to come to life as the sound – like pins being dropped onto glass and coming from his speakers – ceased. He reached into his shoulder bag for another audio cassette, and with the efficiency of an ATC cadet reloading an auto rifle he snapped out the old one, clicked in the new. The pins-on-glass serenade was replaced with another, this time rather akin to number 8 screws being dropped onto a metal tray. Like me he hadn't graduated to CDs. But he probably couldn't afford it, whereas with me the reason was... I had to admit it, that I had begun to resist change.

I leaned forward to peer at the 105mm x 70mm clear plastic box with its slot-in paper cover design. I still hadn't recovered from the move away from 12" vinyl. It was a design of flowers – carnations mainly. In the top right was a colour code bar – the sort of printing convention found at the edge of colour magazines. There was a tab of squares; pink, green, magenta, and at the bottom a half square of yellow. Oddly enough I knew what the flowers were all about. A painting by Henri Fantin-Latour, and I knew that because at art college we'd all had to do a little talk on an artist and – for some weird reason – I'd chosen him. Suddenly the boy opened his eyes, saw me looking.

'New Order…'

I assumed it was an expression for newly arrived stock and that he must be an assistant in a record store. I nodded. He closed his eyes.

But there was a flaw in my plan for today. Why was I sitting here on Southern Railways inhaling that unrefined gas-blood-latrine stench from the defective air conditioning, when I could have been enjoying the mature fustiness of the London Underground? The answer was that my possible future employers were located in a town on the South coast. The commute – even if weekly – would be hell. Sooner, rather than later I would be forced to break the sanctuary of my beloved London W4.

TWO

The forecast had said it was going to be 'a scorcher'. June 20th 1984, the hottest day of the year so far, and just the day for a trip to the seaside. But I had this nagging feeling I was heading in the wrong direction – oh, not the geography, I knew the address, I mean in life.

There's something about a seaside town. I don't just mean the breeze you breathe when you come out of the railway station, nor the sight and sound of gulls. People say 'oohh, it's only *half* a town', but that's just it, that's the frisson. You walk… walk towards the sea. The logical lobe of your brain tells you that when you reach those peeling aqua-painted iron railings you must stop, but the wild imaginative other half of your grey matter wants you to go on, out to sea and up into never-ending space.

I had loads of time before the interview so I didn't need to walk fast but I couldn't help it. Suited, booted, and clutching my brown leather attaché case I could feel myself pumping asphalt which was already as sticky as the surface of sucked rock candy and by the end of the day would be as soft as chewing gum.

The buildings on either side of the street had been painted the craziest colours – no planning permission restrictions here, just chromatic anarchy. Houses near the station were small, so all those stately stucco terraces I'd seen pictures of would have to be nearer the sea. The footpath below me began to slope down, and at the rate I was moving I would arrive at the interview looking as if I'd just stepped out of the spa pump-room Turkish bath.

At last, there it was, the English Channel; big, wet and, considering the atmospheric gusts, surprisingly flat. I was no stranger to the coast but I'd come from the industrial North, a far cry from southern towns of pleasure. I could feel my hair lifting as a breath of ocean-cooled wind made the tiny drops of sweat on my forehead feel like ice.

I sailed on past shops with bow fronts, past pub signs swinging in the flurry, past houses close-boarded, houses clad in shiplap, clapboard, clap-your-hands, bitumened – betch-yer-life… Gawd'struth, s'welp me, shiver-me-timbers I couldn't live here. The pace of it would give me a heart attack. I needed the dead air of London, the never-moving traffic, the miasma of carbon monoxide, and the moribund stench of buddleia in a neglected West London garden.

I walked down the Old Steine, past the pavilion, nosed my way through The Lanes – twee-er than Camden Market and only half as interesting. Soon I found myself in a less salubrious area – not far from the old workhouse, and for the first time it dawned on me that this town had a history which was not exclusively dedicated to pleasure. Just like in my Northern hometown there was unemployment, homelessness, drug addiction, and something else; a high proportion of AIDS, something new and which seemed to be capable of affecting everybody, not just gay men.

The address I'd been given for Promo Designs led me down a narrow alleyway between a dark doorway and one of thirty tattoo emporiums I'd passed since arriving at the railway station. Aberdeen Steak Houses, Airports, Aeroface, Promo's client list was impressive so I was taken aback by its choice of location. The gap between the buildings was sufficiently wide to accommodate me and a dark maroon Volvo which slid past and turned right into a yard in front of me. This was it, The Old Bottle Works.

The image of the dark doorway with its coloured plastic ribbons had released a rather bossy moralistic genie from my brain, and as I tapped my way across the cobbles I wondered how many alcoholics this place had fuelled, how may lives ruined.

I threaded my way through the parked cars; Saabs, Citroen 2CVs, and a surprising number of bicycles. No lift, so up a chequer plate metal stair, through an open wooden door with a hundred coats of paint on it, across hairy smelly matting, and into an over-lit lobby where I fingered a cream plastic intercom.

'It's...' There was a click – which reminded me of the boy on the train with his cassettes.

The firm where I was working at the moment was big – two hundred and fifty of us – but it was in conventional-type offices. You mixed with the people you shared a room with, you saw the walls of the corridors, its ceilings, the boardroom, but you never saw everybody at once. The space I found myself stepping into this morning was like nothing I'd seen before... Three thousand square feet of open plan, a hectic flush of activity, and so much so that I barely noticed the slim cast-iron stanchions holding up the white-painted low-vaulted ceiling.

Everything was maple; maple floor, maple desks, maple cupboards. People were milling everywhere in a state of herd happiness, smiles, teeth, hands gripping hands. There were hi-fives, 'yos', it was a hive of human bees converting the nitty nectar of work a day problems into design honey. Miles Davis's *Bitches Brew* was playing on a hidden tape deck.

My heart banged its way back down the chequer plate stair when I saw six other guys in suits waiting in white Wassily chairs, their Samsonite briefcases resting on the maple. They all looked older than me and were doubtless more experienced. I didn't stand a chance.

'Hiiii, Puuulse – it has to be!' A petite black girl was gripping my hand – shoulder as well, it felt like she was trying to kiss me. She saw me looking at the suits in chairs, saw my face. 'No worrieees, these guys are sales reps,' then in a whisper, 'we call them heat-seeking reps, you know like missiles?' Her voice went up at the end, as if it were a question. 'I'll show you round. Jon-n-Den'll be with you innajiff.'

Funny, half a second ago I'd been worrying about *not* getting the job because of the competition. The news about the heat-seeking reps had slightly dampened my appetite and I had an awful feeling that I was going to be offered the job. Oh, this place was swish all right, it was a managerial position, but it was all bigger than I'd thought. There were sixty people in the room, and I could see all of them at once.

'I'm Tanni bythewayye,' she brushed my fingers with her hand as if she were scattering stardust. 'You can shower here,' she enthused sweeping aside a sliding door and presenting a darkish chamber with wooden duckboards. 'Not nowwe!' She spotted my look of alarm and her hand went back up to my shoulder.

'Guys like to bike in… 5am in summer. We're always at our desks by 0800hrs.' What happened in between? She saw what I was thinking, stepped backwards on the maple and out went the index finger which seemed to be pointing straight at my crotch. 'Power breakfast, right?' Another question – except she was telling me, not asking.

'We sometimes have a shared lunch… Jon-n-Den are super-cheffy – otherwise it's do your own thing, eat *al desko.*' While she was speaking I was watching both of our reflections on the walls. Every section of wall that hadn't got a window in it had been clad with full-height mirror. It felt like being in a gym.

There was no privacy in this office. Brain storming, bubble-diagramming, typing, printing, drawing, coffee-making on the Bosch cappuccino machine; telephoning, canoodling… mmm there'd be plenty of that – I could feel it in the air – would all happen under the public gaze. The place where I worked at the moment had been nicknamed 'The Dating Agency' and I wanted to get away from office politics. This was stylish, but it was more of the same in a different guise.

'Okaaay, Jon-n-Den are hot-to-trot – ready to roll!' Tanni shimmied away to attend to the heat-seeking reps.

Probably because it was transparent I hadn't noticed it before, but right in the middle of the human bustle was a glass box. Glass roof, glass walls, glass door, and it was a sufficiently large space to accommodate a circular white-topped table.

Sitting at the table and opposite one another were two men, one dark curly-haired and wearing a sweatshirt with red and black hoops like Dennis the Menace. The other man was bald, shiny and wore a white shirt open at the neck.

The curly-haired man was my age, the bald one about 40. There was nothing on the table and, as the two appeared to be motionless, I assumed it was a kind of art installation. They saw me, waved, and the bald man's hand movement turned into a 'come hither' with his finger. I pushed, crossed the threshold and closed the glass door behind me. I was surprised how quiet it was after the frenzy outside.

They stood. I'd guessed that 'curly' was Den. He had little dark eyes with V-shaped eyebrows that gave the impression they'd been painted on, like a trainee circus clown. As for 'baldy'... I know this sounds prejudiced, politically incorrect and everything... but I have a dislike of bald men – oh, don't misunderstand me I admire big tall baldies – but this guy stood barely five feet above the maple. He was a white-shirted goblin and as we shook hands I noted that he had the breath of a dragon.

'This is where we hire and fire...' instructed Baldy... Fire? A visit from St George wouldn't come amiss here. '... And if we want to get really nasty...' He nonchalantly produced from his pocket a white remote control, jabbed at one of the buttons and hey presto, the glass walls of the box frosted. I couldn't believe it. In one move we were cocooned in a milk-like substance, invisible to and from the melee outside.

'It's an electric current... changes the molecules in the glass. Same as the ones just installed in the toilet cubicles at Philippe Starck's Café Costes in Paris.' I'd seen the magazine articles and I had to admit it was impressive.

'Have a go.' Baldy lobbed me the remote. I fingered it and watched the crazy scene outside come and go.

'Try the green button.' I pressed. The tabletop started to rotate at the speed of the Telecom Tower restaurant. Red brought it to a stop.

'It's a little game we play when we have our "blue-sky" sessions. We call it thinking *inside* the box.' I gave a chuckle of recognition and felt a bit of a creep.

'I'm Good Cop, and this is Bad Cop,' said Baldy indicating Dennis the Menace. 'But we swap roles sometimes.'

The recently opaqued glass door behind me opened twelve inches.

'It'sonlyme!' The voice was invisible, female, and the kind of 'little girlie' diction which signalled the theatrical.

'Arya reddy for yer teas?' Again, little girlie, but this time parodying a northern skivvy.

Orders were taken through the door giving the procedure a curious air of disembodiment.

We sat at the table; Den on my right, Baldy on my left, and me with my back to the door. Talk was perfunctory and they seemed to have no wish to see my work. Again, the door behind me opened, but wider this time and throwing a shaft of sunlight across the tabletop.

''Eres yer teas!'

… Silence. I half turned to look at the person who had just entered. She was aged about forty, five foot five, slim, with hair the colour of thick-cut marmalade and worn in a mid-length bob. She had a smiling, comfortable kind of face, blue eyes with gold lights and I'd sufficient experience of office life to recognize mischief when I saw it.

She was wearing a good-quality grey-blue plaid wool

skirt, and navy cashmere V-neck pullover worn on top of a white school blouse. Her make-up was understated and she was wearing stockings – yes on a day like this – pale fine denier ones… On her feet were what appeared to be cream ballet pumps which gave me the uncomfortable recollection of last night's dream. God, I felt tired.

She bent forward and placed the black metal tray, with three white half-spherical mugs, on the table – closer to Den than to Baldy and me. I had the slightest glimpse of white garter belt as the wool of her skirt rode up.

'Thank you, Polly.' Den's voice sounded like a tired caress… he'd read my thoughts. 'Her circulation's not good.'

'That's right, it needs frequent massage.' She'd dropped the girlie-speak. It was the sophisticated contralto of an ex-private school and uni graduate.

'That'll be all, Polly,' said Den.

There was a polite cough from Baldy, and a '… for now that is.'

She turned, moving awkwardly and walking from the knee as if she'd recently hurt her back, carefully opened the glass door and closed it behind her.

'… You married, Pulse?' Baldy spoke, eyeing me solemnly as if he was about to hatch a plan.

It was a normal question – particularly for a job interview but I could feel myself blushing. There was Denise, but I didn't want to go into that.

'*We're* both hitched,' volunteered Baldy '… not to one another of course!' He held up his right hand in a 'get-you!' gesture. 'Den the Men' looked at him furiously.

'My kids are at uni – one at Southampton and… t'other at UEA,' persisted Baldy.

The way he pronounced 't'other' was *tuther*. Both of these guys were from the South – smooth, clipped speech, almost certainly ex-private school. Was there a soupçon of mockery going on, or was I being oversensitive?

'Den's kids are still babes… aren't they, Den?' Den's little eyes seemed to take on a renewed bout of fury.

'… So, if we offer you this job… will you be moving out of London?'

This was the bullet I had to bite.

'Well, what I thought I'd do is suck it and see…'

'Oh, we like to do that here don't we… *don't* we, Den?' Baldy was almost shouting that last phrase. There was the sound of a leather shoe sole scraping the maple floor.

'… I thought I'd commute weekly and look for digs – initially, until I've… sucked it – so to speak.' I gave a nervous chuckle and regretted my attempt at banter as the table shook with the impact of Den's shoe against its pedestal.

'Well in that case…' said Baldy clasping his hands together across his stomach, inhaling through his teeth and looking in the direction in which Polly had disappeared. '… I think we should be able to fix you up with something.'

There was a noise as the door thudded closed and I realized that Den had got up and left the glass box.

'Don't mind him; he's all right when you get to know him. We'd very much like you to join us here. Welcome aboard. When can you start?'

THREE

I cowered rather than sat, on the return train journey, hoping very much that I wouldn't run into anybody I knew. There's nothing like being offered a job to give one a moment of elation, but it hadn't lasted. After I left The Old Bottle Works I got an early lunch and went on a longish walk on the all-pebble beach.

By the time I caught the train back to Victoria it was mid afternoon and I was looking forward to standing hugger-mugger on the District Line. Imagine Southern Railways every day? Promo Designs were clearly 'the business', they were slick, had an up-and-coming reputation. It would be a good career move... but I just wasn't happy with the office politics. How long before I fell out with Baldy, how soon before Dennis the Menace blew himself and everybody around him to pieces. I felt depressed.

I ran through a mental to-do list"

- wait for formal job offer to arrive
- give notice – breaking the news to Geoff would be

pleasurable, but not to Ros… 'Judaaasss, I thought we were a team!'

- buy a Southern Railways season ticket
- look for digs… oh *God*, Polly!

I slid the buckle on my attaché case, opened and gazed into it – as one does when one's in the depths… took out the copy of *Building Design* (BD) magazine which had arrived the day before but because of all the excitement I hadn't read it. There were usually several copies in the office but I always had one posted to my flat. There was never time to read it in the office, and anyway… there were office spies.

Anybody seen trawling the classifieds was marked as a potential deserter. They might return to work after daring to take a perfectly innocent week's holiday and find somebody else doing their job… doing it better. There were even mischief-makers who would remove attractive-looking advertised posts, scissoring them from the magazine. It was all fuel for the fire of suspicion.

What with the rhythm and rattle of the train I couldn't concentrate on the articles on Building Regulations, Conservation, and an update on the about-to-open new airport terminal at Birmingham. I cast my eye down the classifieds. Why not? It was no different from buying hi-fi, a suit, a pair of shoes… an attaché case – you still kept looking after you'd made your purchase, just to reassure yourself you'd made the right decision. Then I saw it…

Lloyd Lewis Associates requires office manager for small design practice in North London. Managerial experience essential; salary negotiable…

Patrick Lloyd Lewis had been my hero… well not exactly *hero*, but as a teenager instead of girlie pictures I'd perhaps rather oddly had photos of his work pinned up in my bedroom. He was 'a name' – except nobody really knew that much about him. I'd read somewhere that he'd recently lost his wife.

When I got to Victoria I made straight for the payphones. I was curious, that's all. The article I'd had pinned up on my wall at home in the north of England mentioned that he drove a Jensen, had a house in Cheyne Walk. It had chimed with my desperately undernourished juvenile aspirations.

I put in the 10p piece, dialled the number. It rang out. My watch said 5.45pm; too late, they'd have all gone home. After six rings there was a noise like a full strike in a bowling alley followed by sufficient silence to give me time to clear my throat.

'Lloyd Lewis.' The male voice sounded artificial, plummy – not Eton, more provincial thespian. There was an emptiness about the acoustic at the other end of the phone – as if the voice were coming from a large indoor auditorium, the speaker centre stage, under spotlight.

'I'm interested in your advert for an office manager.' There was another silence and I could hear a tiny fleshy popping sound following by an 'O'.

'And *why*, do you want to come and work here?' The 'why' sounded slightly ridiculous, as if it were spoken for the benefit of an audience which was close to the speaker, not for me standing miles away in a phone booth. It was definitely Shakespearean, as if he was holding a skull in one hand, the clunky black Bakelite telephone handset in the other… Well, if he thought I was going to hesitate he was wrong. I had my elevator pitch ready.

'I work in an office of 250 right now. I want experience running a small office to a high professional standard producing top quality design.' There was a further silence, and in my fantasy, I could visualize him scrutinizing the skull, bringing his popping lips close to its grinning teeth.

'Then you need to come and *see* me.' The emphasis on the 'see' gave the voice the minute tetchiness of the practised and predatory homo.

I fumbled with my Filofax. When? I'd already given Geoff the story of a dead aunt. I would need to rustle up an excuse for *another* day off. If I suggested tomorrow then I could say it was food poisoning from the post-funeral prawn sandwiches.

'I could come tomorrow?'

'...Tomorrow?' The thespianite voice gave the impression that my suggestion had been nothing short of insubordination. 'Come right *now*!'

I suppose I could be there in an hour. It was going to be a long day.

'Err...'

'Tomorrow...' the voice boomed again, 'and... Tomorrow. May be too late!'

FOUR

It was a quarter to seven when I shuffled up the steps of the tube station and across the cool terrazzo floor of a ticket hall flooded with commuters on their way home. A man and a woman were standing on opposite sides of the space selling contrasting political newspapers, each shouting their repetitive slogan.

'Zowjalist Wergar!' The man's voice sounded angry and threatening.

'... Gweene Party!' The woman's cry seemed to be in supplication, as if each were characters singing an ominous duet in an opera. It was a relief to get out into the stifling heat of the street.

Stupid! I hadn't been concentrating and I'd got off a stop too soon. I walked up the hill, past the pub where Ruth Ellis shot her lover, past the enormous church with its fat tower... Derelict for years, but still trying to hang onto the present by its two clocks. Both telling different times, both wrong but *'be right twice a day guv'nor!'* Clocks in high places are too expensive to keep going these days. It's as if the price of reliability has risen beyond our means. Two days previously I'd read about five thousand police who'd taken on a group of 'rioting South Yorkshire miners'. Why was it that the streets of the South – particularly certain parts of London – seemed to be paved with soft gold?

I assumed that I knew this area because I'd been here before. It was twelve years ago while at college in the North, and I'd got myself a summer job in an architect's office. Mum had almost passed out when I told her. She'd never been to London. I got digs in a big house... owner was an artist, spent most of his time in Spain so I had the attic – two cavernous rooms. I always got up early and – unless it was raining – walked over Primrose Hill into Gloucester Place. The other guys in the office thought I was mad.

Funny how memory presses in upon you... Not with the stuff you can recall, but with what you *can't*. Look once and you think you've got the hang of things, look again and you find that the world is very different to what you thought.

The houses I remembered round here were huge – detached, with red brick that looked as if it had been dusted in paprika. There had been neglected gardens, pointy roofs and clumpy terracotta gateposts whose tops were spiky like the helmets of Genghis Khan's soldiers. The house I was standing in front of today was completely different to what I'd imagined.

It was the end of a row of twelve, a five-storey terrace, and 'perfect' in the sense that all houses were virtually identical. Sulphur-yellow brick, sticky black-painted iron railings – gates and balconies encrusted with ferrous flowers. I guessed at 1785. It looked like the wing of a country house of that date.

But there was something wrong. The other wing – and the centre section which no doubt had been intended to have stone columns and pediment – was missing. What lay beyond the last house in the terrace were more of the paprika-dusted pointy roofed homes which had been built a century later.

Something had put a premature end to this architectural development. I could only speculate. Time and money are the usual reasons for abandoned projects, but in those days disease and sudden death were just as likely. Cholera was always a creeping shadow.

I was soaking. The walk from the tube station had made me feel as if I'd just stepped out of a hot bath, and the humidity inside my trousers was making the hairs on my legs prickle. I'd unwound my tie while swaying along on the tube, shrugged off my jacket as I padded up the hill. My attaché case felt as if it had changed back into the bovine creature from which it had been crafted, and the metal core of its handle was biting into my right hand. I'd threaded my jacket through the handle and it looked rather naff, like those touristy people who walk around with the arms of their pullovers tied round their waists.

Each property of the terrace had two steps leading up to the front door, and I could see more steps disappearing down to the right – no doubt leading to cellars. I looked for a nameplate but there was nothing except a wrought-iron bell which felt surprisingly cool to my fingers. It was in the form of a bull's head, and in order to pull it I had to grasp the bull's horns.

I stepped back and stood still long enough to feel the sun burning my left cheek before the black shiny door swung inwards. I was blinded, the space beyond the door was a rectangle of dark and I could see nothing except a hand holding a sparkling tumbler of water. I stood there like a mirage-hallucinating Bedouin.

'*You* look hot, you'll need this!' The voice was female, deep – almost *tessitura*. I put my attaché case down, took the glass in my right hand and practically downed it in one. I was parched – hadn't got used to this new habit of carrying bottled water, and gulped at it, conscious of my Adam's apple welting away.

'Cheers!' I couldn't think of anything more imaginative to say.

An aircraft passed in front of the sun and for a split second I caught sight of my benefactor…Tallish, slim, and hair worn in a dark bob.

'I'm Pulse… Interview.' As I moved forward out of the sun I could see that she was dressed in the manner of the waitress of a pre-war tearoom; white blouse, black skirt, black stockings, patent shoes – some kind of crossover strap black top. I didn't offer my hand because I assumed she was a domestic servant. Instead I picked up my attaché case and followed her inside.

'You saved my life,' I tittered wetly as she took the tumbler from my hand. I suddenly realized how cold it was in the house, the chilled water sloshing around in my stomach made me shiver and I reached for my jacket.

Outside on the steps and away from the traffic it had seemed quiet, while in here there was a curious echo from the stone floor and bare white-painted plaster walls. I was conscious of a smell coming from somewhere, something not nice… Not the usual drain smell, this was a stench.

I had never eaten pheasant, nor had I ever smelt it. My mum and dad had always assumed that that kind of food was not for their class of people. We weren't country folk and I'd never taken the initiative to try it for myself. But I'd read that it needed to be well hung. '*Under-hung poultry is for the bourgeoisie…*' the article had said, '*the posher you are, the longer you hang it, and if you're really upper class you get your servants to pick the maggots out of it.*' This was what I imagined well-hung pheasant might smell like… rotten, even gangrenous.

'Mr Lloyd Lewis will see you shortly.' The contrast with this morning's trendy little adventure made me want to giggle. Surely life here couldn't be *that* formal? I followed the woman along the hall towards – on the left – a stone stair leading up, and – to the right – a narrower corridor with two steps leading down to the rear of the house. She turned to her right and steered me into a large light-filled room, and for the first time I could see her face; features dignified but pale. There was a small purplish bruise on the flesh under her right ear.

The room I found myself in was like many London townhouses in that the wall dividing front reception room from rear had been removed making a serviceable studio. There were four pale-green drawing boards, white work trolleys, and black upholstered drafting stools. In the rear half of the room several tables had been put together to form a conference table. Like the hall, the walls were naked painted plaster, and as I shifted my feet looking for somewhere to put my attaché case, my boots clonked on timber boards stained the colour of molasses. Somewhere above my head a door slammed violently.

The woman put the glass tumbler down on the nearest desktop. 'I need to close the shutters,' she said as if she'd received an invisible order.

She moved towards the two tall windows which faced the street and where the shutters, consisting of four stripped wooden panels, hung in pairs. Each pair met in the middle and when standing open they stacked like a concertina. While she folded the panels of the right-hand window, I peered through the left one. There was a sound from above like someone dropping a heavy piece of furniture.

The woman gently bumped each shutter leaf until they met in the middle. She clanged the black-painted metal arm across the closed leaves where it clicked home into its metallic partner. When she repeated the process with the second window I turned and moved towards the rear part of the room where there was a single window of similar width and height.

Through the window and one storey below I glimpsed the grey-green fuzz of a neglected garden; threadbare lawn, smashed terracotta pots and tangled buddleia. I could see an old wooden bench, which judging from its size might have been fashioned for a performance of *Parsifal*. There was a hollow thud from above as if someone had collapsed onto the floor.

'Patrick needs a little longer,' she said as she dropped the final metal shutter arm into place and the room was shrouded in near darkness. My watch said 7.30 and I didn't have anything planned, but it had already been a long day and I was still suffering from the after effects of the dream. I was beginning to regret having come.

The room had the sensation of no work having taken place in it for years. There were no noticeboards, no calendars, no Post-it notes, not a pencil out of place. Each desk had a shiny black telephone – the coiled wire between phone and handset all facing the same way.

Though the objects themselves were redolent of a modern office, the way they had been arranged spoke of the cells of monks, and possessed all the quirkiness of contraptions used by medieval scribes as might be seen on the vellum of illuminated manuscripts. The smell of rank poultry seemed worse than ever.

'Leave your case where it is.' Her voice had taken on a curtness that made my buttocks tingle inside my boxer shorts, and as I followed her from darkened room into gloomy hall I had the disconcerting feeling that I was no longer in control of events, they were controlling me.

I followed along the stone corridor onto the stair head where the woman began stepping carefully down a flight of worn treads leading to the basement. I waited until the top of her bobbed head was level with my waist before I did likewise. We were in perfect step with one another, as if we were only one person descending to an unknown region. I heard another thump from above – and something else I was unable to identify, something shrill.

The hum I could hear below me was coming from a large photocopying machine in an alcove directly opposite the bottom of the stair. From ahead I could hear the metallic trilling of a fridge, and the soft tinkling of water bottles. The woman must have been down here when I had pulled on the bull's head bell.

She led me into a large low space, the footprint of the one above, its walls painted but instead of smooth plaster they were rough brick. The crannies and crevices within hinted at further unexplored spaces behind, as if there were somehow two worlds here, one visible, the other hidden.

The main source of light was from a window in the rear wall beneath which stood a white table the size of four doors laid flat. Whatever happened down here clearly took place round this table.

'Samples library...' She was looking at me closely, watching my every response. I could see it now, *Sanderson, Liberty, Bruno Triplet, Zimmer & Rhodes*; fabrics, they were all there, folded on shelves and hanging from racks, while on the lower shelves were carpet fragments, tufted, loop pile, sisal, and coir. There was an extensive section of hard finishes; ceramic tiles, porcelain, marble, thermoplastic, real linoleum. I was used to working with materials like this and for a moment my anxiety lessened. A smell of linseed oil hung in the air and briefly I forgot the stench of fowl.

Through the rear window I could see the garden, and in that strange ethereal light one experiences in a north-facing garden at 7.45pm after a blindingly hot day, the *Parsifal* bench looked odder than ever. Just under the front lip of its seat was an inscription which looked as if it had been burnt into the surface of the wood with a cattle branding iron; *CARVED FROM THE TIMBERS OF HMS BLOODAXE.* I turned to face the woman, half expecting an explanation but she seemed to be intent only on watching me. Her demeanour was of domestic servant but I had the uncanny feeling that inside lurked something with a greater authority.

As she moved back to the centre of the room my eye was caught by a dark fret-cut Oriental screen, through which I could see daylight coming from the front window. Why was there a fully made-up double bed behind the screen? My eye was distracted as my ear was entrapped by a scraping sound coming from the subterranean area outside, and I had the fleeting impression of a human form passing the window.

The woman led me out of the room and along the corridor to the rear of the building. Behind me I could hear feet grittily stamping up the outside front steps, the rasping of a key in the front door above our heads, followed by squeaking shoes and the sound of something being dragged across the stone floor.

At the end of the corridor I could see a door. The woman opened, entered, and held it so I could follow. The space inside measured four feet by eight and appeared to contain nothing more than a toilet and washbasin. She indicated that I should close the door behind us, and as I did so I noticed that hanging on the wall behind the door was a bicycle whose shiny metal pedals looked virgin. I'd been a keen cyclist and in an inexplicable gesture my left forefinger and thumb gently squeezed the bike's chain. As I looked at the drizzle of clear oil which had oozed onto my index finger I realized how uneasy I felt standing so close to the woman in somewhere which had been designed as a place of privacy for one person.

Without sound or warning she reached behind her and grasped what looked like a crowbar. I recoiled, and in stepping backwards noticed beneath my feet the distinct line of an inspection chamber. She placed her legs apart – feet firmly planted on the tiles, and with the clanging a tram makes as it passes over a rail junction she prised away the two-inch thick lid releasing the source of the stench.

'The Canal!' Her voice had acquired the sonority of a Russian Orthodox priest in full incantation.

'But we're on a hill... I didn't know there was a canal.' I leaned forward, gagged and turned away trying to disguise it as a cough. Attempting not to breathe I looked back and down into blackness slicked with tiny silver lights.

'... London's twenty-seven lost rivers, it's one of them.' She looked at me sharply as if I should have known. 'When they were tunnelling for King's Cross railway station they canalized it.' I tried to picture the procession of torch-lit narrow boats, bargees lying on outstretched planks and 'driving' the boat with their feet while the horses were led over the surface.

I wondered about offering to help her replace the heavy cover but she clearly had her own way of doing it. For a moment I thought I heard a roaring – not from below but coming from way above. It was the kind of bellowing some bovine creature might make.

'Mr Lloyd Lewis will see you now.'

FIVE

'Mr Lloyd Lewis will see you *now*.' The emphasis was on the last word.

Assuming that she would be escorting me upstairs I walked to the bottom of the stone steps and waited.

'Up two flights, through the door on the left and it's the door straight in front of you... don't forget to knock on the second door.'

It was eight o'clock as I walked back up the stairs to the ground floor, along the hall corridor, and while running my right index finger up the curved wooden handrail I tentatively tapped up the stone steps towards the first floor. I'd got halfway up the first flight when I realized that my attaché case was still where I'd left it on the floor of the main studio. I pussyfooted back down and retraced my steps at double speed feeling that now I was late.

At the top of the first flight I paused. The stone stair continued up to further floors while to my left I could see a wood-panelled door standing one foot ajar. I pushed without knocking – exactly as I had been told, crossed the threshold from stone onto thick grey carpet and found myself in a small anteroom which contained a dark Jacobean-style wooden chest and two club chairs upholstered in deep-buttoned leather the colour of dried blood.

The walls were painted in a substance unknown to me which seemed to give the room the kind of luminescence of which one was unsure just what was wall, and what might be space beyond. Hovering in front of the walls were three tapestries; the first in blue silks was of a woman examining her face in a handmirror, the second showed a bull's head, while a third depicted a unicorn being devoured by a lion and a bull while being observed by a dog, a monkey, and a trio of rabbits. As I leaned forward to get a closer look at the third hanging a floorboard creaked beneath the carpet upon which I was standing and I was conscious of another sound, a faint groaning which seemed to come from the room beyond.

I'd been so engrossed in the tapestries that I'd failed to notice that the final door was standing wide open. Through the opening I could see three tall *piano-nobile* windows in the front of the house. The low sun gave the room beyond the feeling of silent incandescence, and the foliage across the road the strange appearance of honey fungus.

I was so bewitched that I'd taken three steps into the room before I was aware I'd forgotten to knock. It seemed deserted except for a giant elaborately decorated walnut desk behind which hung a further tapestry covering the entire wall.

The tapestry's centrepiece was a lady wearing a conical headdress and standing in front of a pointed tent decorated with blue fleurs-de-lis. She was being attended by a smaller female who was holding open the lid of a carved casket. On the right of the composition was a unicorn, rearing on hind legs, while to the left of the picture was a lion also rampant and in the act of pawing at the cloak of the principle lady. Before I could retrace my steps in order to knock, I saw that I was not alone in the room.

Seated behind the desk but turned sideways and leaning forward so that his salt-and-pepper-haired head seemed to be about to disappear into the mouth of the lion was a man. His face was obscured by his hands.

As if on cue he turned towards me and still remaining seated he murmured as if to some other unseen person who was also in the room, 'I was just having a few moments alone with my late wife.'

'Yes, of course!' I mouthed – the 'yes' came out like the sound from a distressed Chihuahua, the 'of course' as if to reassure him that it was perfectly normal for job interviews to be preceded by a short period of devotions for the departed.

After a further interval while I stood feeling like an intruder he got up, stamped round the walnut monster and held out his hand.

'Patrick Lloyd Lewis!' He said it exactly like the returning officer announcing the election results at a town hall – '*Patrick Lloyd Lewis (Conservative)…*'

The man in front of me was five-foot nine, stocky with a thick neck, and wearing a navy club blazer, diagonally striped tie, grey worsted trousers, and black highly polished brogues. As his hand snapped shut on mine I found it difficult to meet his eyes, both iris and pupil seemed to be entirely black.

'Sit down, Pulse,' – he pronounced it *Palse* – 'and tell me *all* about yourself.' He gestured towards the wooden-seated captain's chair on 'my' side of the great walnut barrier reef. His was a high-backed swivel chair upholstered in deep-buttoned leather the colour of dock leaves, and his '*all about myself*' sounded like a statement of intent and that he would be satisfied with nothing less than my entire life story.

'Well, I've been working…'

'I'm fifty-eight,' he cut in as if it were the prelude to a proposal of marriage, the subtext of which might be – *and quite youthful with it wouldn't you say?* Come to think of it his face did have a young look, but the flat nose, the wide chin gave it a kind of subcutaneous juvenility as if it was capable if renewing itself every so often in the way that a chelonian might shed its skin. There was a perceptible whiff of cologne.

'Well, I've been working…'

'They sometimes call me Probus you know.' As he pronounced the 'O' I heard the familiar lip-sucking noise I'd identified over the telephone at Victoria station.

There was a soft tap at the door and the woman entered, gliding towards the walnut fortress. In her right hand were several freshly typed letters which she placed in front of Patrick, setting them down on a large pad of white blotting paper its edges bound in black leather. He leaned backwards, while the dock-leaf chair leather creaked under the strain. His lips resumed the 'O' shape, but it was no longer the moist naughtiness of '*they call me Probus*', there was something dangerous in the expression. The mouth had taken on the dark fissured texture of the anus of some unknown creature.

The woman remained standing, while the man's right hand reached for the maroon *Mont Blanc* – an elongated egg of a fountain pen which was resting impertinently alongside the blotting pad. The eyes gave a vatic glare towards the woman as wedge-shaped fingers twisted the cap off the pen. He gave each letter perfunctory scrutiny and with an almost comical flourish signed them, the pen making the near inaudible sound of ink and metal on ever-so-slightly textured cream notepaper. He held them out for the woman to take.

'I told you to include the consultants on the distribution lists. Do them all again – *now*!' The voice was a bellow. Without expression the woman took the letters and left the room.

'Lauren,' – *Lawrrahn* he pronounced it – 'she's a star...' He enthused like a conductor introducing his soloist, as he looked at the doorway she'd recently walked through '... *absolute* star! She's a baroness you know...' he announced turning back to fix me with his pupils – dark as the ink he'd just used to sign the useless letters, '... Hereditary, not life. Since her old father died she's been all on her own.'

I could feel the vatic glare on *me* now. It was as if I was being given a set of instructions and for the first time I realized that Lauren was about my age.

While the signing had been in progress I'd taken the opportunity to delve into my attaché case and take out my portfolio, all in compact A4 format.

'Oh, so you've brought *something* to show me.'

I opened it at a very detailed pencil working drawing, a cross-section through a reception desk I'd designed for an advertising agency. I was particularly proud of the piece.

Again, there was a light tap on the door. I thought it was Lauren... in fact I did a double take. The woman standing there seemed to be Lauren but *wasn't* Lauren.

'Ah Martiniqua! This is Pulse. He's showing me his work and look...' he jabbed his wedge-shaped digits at the drawing of the reception desk, '... he's been good enough to bring me items of unfinished work. Come!' He gestured to Martinique to take up position behind his right shoulder.

'You see, Martinique...' he continued, index and second finger resting across my drawing and tapping it twice. 'This is what *we* in the business call *pencilling in*.' He pronounced each vowel and consonant as if he were speaking to a three-year-old.

'Patrick, I've got a meeting at the UN this evening, my driver's coming in fifteen minutes.' She spoke in rapid clipped English monotone with an accent I guessed was French. She was wearing a magenta-coloured business suit which had a slight emphasis at the shoulders.

'...That's in Whitehall, by the way,' she added in a whispered *in case you didn't know* tone, close to his pink little ear and while stroking the back of her hand across his shoulder. Her eyes adopted an 'in conference' mode while his wedge-shaped fingers drummed rhythmically against the acetate sleeve of my portfolio and his mouth formed an 'O', but less aggressively this time.

When she'd gone, he simply said, 'Pulse, when can you join us?' I loved the '*us*'.

As I packed up my folio and rose from the chair my eye fell upon an oak-framed colour photograph sitting on an antique Georgian blanket box, I hadn't noticed before. It showed a woman with brunette bobbed hair, skinny scarlet jeans, and a bright pink cotton top with white Aztec pattern. It took no more than a split second to make the connection and unable to stop myself I moved towards it. He saw me staring.

'... My late wife.' He said it petulantly as if it should have been obvious to me.

'What was her name?' I couldn't help myself. Oh God, it was none of my business but I could feel the thrill running through my duodenum. I knew the answer.

He spoke it like the automated message on an answerphone, 'Freia, it's spelled the German way.'

SIX

It had been no contest.

There were two reasons why I'd accepted the job with Patrick, and as I strap-hung on the District Line breathing the bouquet of carbon and halitosis, I compared them. It still wasn't too late – well it probably was now, I'd made my decision, worked my notice and I wasn't going back on my word. It was Monday July 23rd and I was on my way to my first day as manager.

First up had been curiosity – rather like with the payphone in Victoria station, only now the feeling was a hundred times more intense. I'd had *déjà vu* before – we've all had it to some extent but this *had* to be paranormal. The dream had been so clear, then the photograph!

Then there was Patrick. Jesus, the guy was a manipulative rogue if ever I saw one!

I'd consulted my circle of friends. There'd been rumours; Patrick and his wife had split months before her death – though nobody had been sure exactly when that had been, nor how she'd died. At least one story chimed with my nightmare suggesting that she and her new boyfriend had died in a car crash 'somewhere abroad', but other avenues of gossip included a brain haemorrhage, heart attack, breast cancer, and choking on a pistachio nut.

In at least one respect I was mad. Promo Designs was a slick operation, it would have been a good career move, but I felt driven to seek the truth... Except what *was* the truth? Was it my suspicions, rumour based on what I heard from others, or was it fact, the kind of fact to be obtained only by qualified people such as police? I knew very well that I wasn't the person to embark on a full investigation but at the same time I felt I had no choice, I was being drawn into something. The truth would rise to the surface – as by a process of osmosis merely through my presence at Lloyd Lewis Associates.

'Ooze bundle-o-joy is this?' The words manhandled me out of my thoughts as a tall uniformed and capped man followed me onto the train at Bank station and was pushing his way down the crowded car identifying items of anonymous luggage which stood by doors. He pointed at a jumbo khaki sausage of a holdall capable of carrying a human body let alone a bomb. A sheepish studenty young man raised his hand.

'You're meant to put it theya, not *'ear*!' He pointed to the end of the car, and then to the sign above the heads of the strap-hangers, '...Seyz so!' There was nowhere else the *studie* could have put it, and as the doors opened at Old Street he hauled his human-sized bale out of the car onto the platform. The doors closed and the train moved off leaving him standing waiting for the next – perhaps less crowded – train.

The second reason – though no less emotionally inspired – was more complex. For all its eccentricities Lloyd Lewis

Associates seemed to offer an opportunity. Patrick would get the work in, I would hire and fire, I would turn it round. He would make me associate director – okay, his initial response to that hadn't been too positive but I would work on him. Promo was predictable, it was the popular perception of what being a designer was all about and for me destined to be ultimately dull, so here I was.

As a boy I'd done well – failed the eleven-plus but at thirteen picked up a scholarship to the local boys' grammar. I got to be top of the class, there seemed no stopping me, and Mum and Dad fled into their shells in awe of just what kind of erudite only child they'd brought into this world. Dad wanted me to leave school after O Levels, take 'a good clerking position at Swifts', the coach works where he was night watchman… 'summat ta be proud of.' I wanted to go to art college which needed two A Levels, Mum was all for it so in the end we agreed on a compromise, A Levels in one year at the local tech college – which I did, followed by Art Foundation course, and I got into Leeds – my first choice. Dad was jealous but had to lump it.

It was while I was at Leeds that I got the holiday job in London. I wanted Mum and Dad to come and visit me. Dad wouldn't, it would have meant time off. Mum did, she bought a hat, and when I met her off the coach in Victoria I realized that, although I'd seen photos of her in a hat – her wedding, my christening and so forth – this was the first time I'd seen her in anything but rollers or headscarf.

At the Spanish artist's house, I slept in the attic room where the boiler was, Mum in the other room. She was ultra nervous about everything, so when I took her to Flanagan's in Baker Street she thought it was 'a dive' with its sawdust on the floor, waiters in striped kitchen aprons and boaters, until she realized it was deliberate, new, fashionable, and she began to try and relax.

I was showing off – playing the *bon viveur*, it was the first time I'd ever had any cash to spend and I tucked in to cockles, game pie, and treacle suet pud… I think I even had half a bottle of stout. I can't recall what Mum had. Afterwards I took her to a performance of *A Midsummer Night's Dream* – outdoors in Regents Park.

In the final scenes after Oberon has blessed the three couples, all the other characters have left the stage, and Puck suggests to the audience that what they have just experienced may be nothing but a dream, I could see tears rolling down Mum's cheeks. 'No… it's magical, love,' she was almost apologetic, but as we clapped our hands with the five hundred other people in the park that evening we both knew only too well what a dream was. When we got back to the Spanish artist's house I brought up the cockles, game pie, treacle suet pud, and bottle of stout in the downstairs toilet.

Our street – where I lived with my mum and dad – was only half a street. There were twelve red-brick terraced houses – six either side, two-up two-downs with the front door leading straight onto the pavement. Sometime, someone had built a wall across the road. It was so high that even looking out of the window of Mum and Dad's bedroom I could only see the tops of the houses – little conical roofs disappearing into the distance. There were other children in the street with whom I played, and whose parents' bedrooms we could sneak into, but nobody could ever really see what was on the other side of the wall. We'd tried to walk round there to look but for some reason always ended up getting lost. I'd asked Mum, she just shook her head.

I was the smallest child in our little street gang and also the lightest, so when we made a human tower one day it was me who had to go on top. I climbed onto the shoulders of the highest boy, grabbed the smooth warm tiles of the sloping parapet, threw my leg over and sat there triumphantly.

'What can you see?' they were shouting.

'Just houses…' I yelled back, '…they're *just* houses.' But what I didn't tell them was that the houses looked different. They had bay windows; tiny front gardens, ornamental metal gates, and between the pavement and the road there was a strip of green mown grass.

When I told Mum about Lloyd Lewis Associates on the phone – and I always told her everything – she said 'Oh, love, you could really make something of yourself there! If only your dad could have…'

It was just the two of us; Lauren and me sitting at the white laminate-topped conference table in Patrick's office at 11.00am; me facing the window, Lauren opposite. The doors to the anteroom and stone landing were standing open and we were waiting and listening. Lauren had said that we *had* to be there on the dot. I'd arrived at the house well before nine so that had given me plenty of time to get settled in. I'd chosen the drawing board by the window facing out towards the trees, but as I sat and looked out I felt anything but settled.

It was raining, a church clock was striking somewhere in the distance, and as it reached its final stroke it made a duet with the rattle of a Chubb lock being released from somewhere on high within the house. Lauren had told me that Patrick and Martinique had a flat which occupied the top two floors of the house, and it seemed also that Patrick's three children and Martinique's son frequently put in appearances in the house. It was going to be interesting.

I heard the sound of a door opening at the top of the landing. Almost immediately it closed, I could hear something which resembled the ticking of an old grandfather clock and I recalled the black polished brogues and the stone steps. Someone was descending. Through the window I could see a cat sitting on the balcony in front of the decorative ironwork, waiting to be let in. It was the largest domestic cat I'd ever seen and with its black and silver stripes it resembled a giant furry mackerel. I wondered how it had got there in the first place.

The ticking clock ceased, and the floorboard I recalled which had creaked just before my interview, creaked again.

'Typical English weather!' The male voice snapped as if it was not suffering fools gladly.

'Oh, Patrick... your eye! What happened?' Lauren sounded emotional.

I turned, rising as I did – my hand outstretched to greet. The figure which had entered the room was dressed exactly as I had seen it a month ago – except I was sure that now the stripes of the club tie were running right-to-left instead of left-to-right. But there was something extraordinary. Patrick's right eye was concealed behind a pad of blindingly white lint, upholstered with cotton wool and fastened across the face with clear medical tape.

'It's nothing!' He raised his right hand as if in benediction.
'But what happened?'

'My grandson did it.' He sniffed through his flattened nose, pouted his lips and sat down in mystifying silence. The offence was no doubt in the process of being dealt with by law, and Patrick was almost certainly struggling to come to terms with the nature of such a filial crime.

'But he's only two!'

The cat on the balcony put its face a nudge away from the glass of the window. Its head looked like a rather damp striped medicine ball.

Patrick, it transpired, had been to Pizza Express with Jen, one of his daughters, and her two-year old. Somehow the infant had taken possession of the menu – slashing the air around it with laminated plastic. I winced at the vision of pepperoni, sloppy Giuseppe, and sliced human cornea.

'Are you settling in?' He one-eyed me.

'Very well,' I lied. He sounded as if he didn't give a shiny shoe either way.

'I've got something *very* interesting for you, a client in *your* neck of the woods.' He studied me with his cyclopean eye. He hadn't a clue where my neck of the woods was, I hadn't told him, and he'd never even looked at my CV.

The telephone on the walnut desk rang.

'Get that would you.'

Lauren rose, walked to the desk, picked up the receiver.

'Lloyd Lewis Associates…' Her voice was an echo of his (*Conservative*).

'Tell me, Pulse, do you drive around London?' I didn't, I used public transport.

'It's for you, Patrick.' Lauren stood holding the handset, but she was looking in my direction as if there was a hidden message somewhere for me.

Patrick rose, walked to the desk, picked up the phone. I could see the trace of a smile on Lauren's face.

'Lloyd Lewis.'

'I'm doing the drawings right now.' His voice was curt.

'Yes.'… Slightly less curt.

'Yes, promise.'

'Pro-mise…' I sensed a touch of supplication in his voice.

There was the clunk of plastic on finely polished wood as he dropped the receiver onto the tabletop then scooped it back onto the handset. He returned to the head of the table, making a dusting motion with his hands as he sat down.

'My mother's kitchen…' He said it as if he were talking about someone who was having to undergo repeat surgery for a rare and probably incurable condition. I wondered whether she would ever see it finished. He continued.

'You're familiar with GI Group.' It was rhetorical. I wasn't.

'Bicycles, domestic cookers – old tech. They want to get rid of their metal-bashing image. I want you to go take a brief.'

'Aren't you coming?'

'The No-o-o-orth of England!' He pronounced the 'o' with an elongated shudder.

'Can I take Lauren?'

'Certainly *not*!'

It was agreed that I would go tomorrow, on the train.

An inland north-west town – as I gather they used to say in radio announcements during the war, and in point of fact some considerable miles north-west of my neck of the woods. I was looking forward to it.

'… Fancy going for a drink later?' When I was back downstairs Lauren's voice was a mock-conspiratorial whisper.

'…Ye-es, okay!'

I was looking forward to that as well.

SEVEN

It had stopped raining and there was a glimmer of sun behind low cloud. The air seemed to have acquired a new density of heat and as we walked uphill into the wynds above the house, it seemed almost as if it were releasing its special scents; jasmine, mock orange, and honeysuckle.

The Stag and... 'something' Lauren had said. I hadn't got the measure of her at all. A month ago, she'd looked every bit the domestic servant, today she'd refined the image into a John Lewis sales assistant; black skirt, black stockings, patent shoes, and in spite of the warm weather a close-fitting grey cotton turtleneck. There was something I liked about her, at the same time I got the feeling she was out to impress, lighting her little fires, always creating a smoke of mystery.

In the space of the few minutes it took us to reach the pub she'd confided that there was a nuclear submarine stuck under the North Pole which 'could go up any time', that she'd got information about the Russian economy which could have a catastrophic effect on the UK stock market, that she had been party to information that a previous Chancellor of the Exchequer had had his wife murdered. The Lord

Lucanish rumours seemed childish – but you know, even nursery rhymes can prove unsettling to an adult and it all served to increase my general feeling of unease. Whatever the case, it appeared that Lauren saw 'information' as her currency. It was going to be an interesting hour or so. Given the circumstances of my being at Lloyd Lewis Associates in the first place I found the third piece of her information particularly off-putting.

The pub was Edwardian – outside it was all orange rubbed brick and glazed chocolate-coloured tiles. There was a sense of candy-coloured artificiality about everything. Perhaps it was the warm air, the condensation of heavy scents, and the glittering from the stippled glass windows… Perhaps it was just the feeling of first day in a new job? On the pavement stood an 'A' blackboard chalked with the message '*no live music, no jukebox… perfect peace!*' The place would be deserted. I was wrong, it was heaving.

In the hot beery fug of the saloon there was a crazy mix of people; black leather, mangled denim, and parti-coloured hair, while in the lounge I glimpsed a conglobation of club blazers, and the glimmer of white hair.

'I'm having a pint of Fullers ESP!' She spoke loudly. One or two heads turned.

'Of course…' I acknowledged.

'No, *I'll* get them, you find a quiet corner – near the stairs is best.'

'… I'll have the same,' I answered feeling a bit useless.

'Grab hold of this!' She was carrying two shoulder bags, one stuffed inside the other. She removed the inner bag, draped it over her right shoulder and handed me the larger bag with her left. I noticed she was wearing an impressive ring – a huge chunk of amber in a silver setting with a tiny fly which had been trapped within the resin, perhaps millions of years ago.

I took the bag and wove my way through the talking heads. She was right, the crowd was thinner nearer the stairs and I found two seats on a banquette – no stools nearby so no fear of anyone wanting to come and join us. I was familiar with Fullers Extra Special Pride but as I had spent at least some part of every day over the last month wondering as to whether I possessed powers of clairvoyance the ESP bit was making me feel apprehensive.

As I placed Lauren's bag on the banquette next to me I caught sight of white headed notepaper protruding an inch; I couldn't resist giving it a tug; *The Rt Hon Lauren…* there was a printed coat of arms; shield, two rampant lions, basinet, and at least two curly mottos – all I had time to look at before she hove into view with two glasses each containing the shining gold translucent liquid, not a bubble in sight. I smiled, not at the beer but at what I'd seen in the bag.

'You like the décor, I see?'

'Oh… yes.'

The walls had been painted in faux Aberdeen granite, and the staircase looked as if every woodcarver in Edwardian London had worked on it. Mounted – in rows one above the other – against the 'granite' were a hundred stags' heads; the largest in the top row and each with full antlers. Someone had taped a handwritten notice to the bulging balustrade. It read – *This evening's meeting of the Loyal Order of Moose has been cancelled.* I was surprised at their loyalty in booking such a place, given the overwhelming evidence of the cervine massacre which had taken place.

Lauren sat down.

'Patrick isn't *all* shit.'

'Sure…'

'He's a good designer, hmm…' I knew that, but why the sudden directness?

'He likes to think of himself as an aesthetic voluptuary of the highest order, a *Rococo apogee,* yes.'

I wasn't at all ready for this florid character study of Patrick. For one thing I was struggling to adjust to the odd surroundings.

'… But when it comes to ancestral pedigree you may as well know right now that he's all fake hmm.' It didn't surprise me – the thespian accent, the patronising manner.

'The Welsh/Irish aristocracy bit is total crap as well. His father was Felt, hmm…'

My face must have looked as if she'd just put her hand on my knee. '…Phil Felt from Feltham – Veldt probably… Dutch refugees in the sixteenth century.' I took this with a pinch of salt; she made him sound like a character out of an Ian Dury song. I decided not to ask how she knew this.

'Has he any brothers or sisters?'

'Della.'

'Della,' I repeated stupidly.

'… Lives in Canada… older, couldn't wait to clear off from the family. They loathe one another's guts but she comes… every three years, yes… Stays in her room all the time under the pretence of being ill – being brought Rennies, nail varnish, and the *Daily Mail* by Al, Patrick's son. As soon as she gets an invite up she gets, out she goes.'

'Della Felt?'

'Della Duckworth, Duckworth's deceased. It's hilarious

that he chose Lloyd Lewis, it's sooo very like Lloyd Loom – you know – the chairs, yes… He's got them on his roof terrace… He doesn't make a penny out of design, nobody can, that's one of the long list of myths of the world… Makes it on property – and a few other things of course, hmm – owns several places in London, villa in the Ca-*nar*ies…' she was counting on her fingers, '… and France of course.'

'Oh yes, Martinique?'

'No, it's his. Martinique didn't have a thing – zero.' She made an 'O' sign with her finger and thumb. '… Rags to riches… Father was a coal miner in northern France; mine closed, family moved to Toulouse, dad eked out an existence repairing furniture, yes. Martinique… bright, married a uni lecturer – marriage went bust when she met Patrick. Adultery, so *he* got custody of Laurie now seventeen – neither she nor the husband Catholic. Laurie lives with his dad in Marseilles, obviously loves his mum – in fact if you want to know the two of them are as thick as thieves, he's always at the house, hmm!'

'… Really? So… now she's at the UN?'

'Ohh ye-yes… She bright cookie – far brighter than 'Is Nibs. The annual performance prize, *she* won it… Up on the podium giving her little speech, Patrick was there *of course,* and what does he do? He *has* to chip in with, "I refer to that certain phrase, well known even before it appeared in the *Port Arthur News* in 1946… '…*they say that behind every great man there is a woman*…' what the journalist forgot to add is that behind every great woman there is a great man." You can imagine everybody laughed but that's what *he actually* believes.' I didn't ask her how she knew all that either.

'How about you?' At last she asked.

'Well, I've been working…'

'It's not all plain sailing with Martinique either,' she cut in. 'Not her, she hasn't the time; it's him.'

'What?'

'Put it this way, "lady's man" isn't a term that Patrick would approve of, hmm. He'd prefer you to think of him as the possessor of a deep and rich understanding of women; rather like his deep and rich understanding of wine – you've got all that bit to come… So, you've been working where? Patrick didn't say.'

'I've been working…'

'Have you noticed how he can waggle each of his ears separately? He's particularly proud of his eyebrows, hmm. Leonine, he thinks they are, except if you look closely at a lion's eyebrows they're practically non-existent. So are those of a bull… So, all this stuff about him being "like a bull" is *complete bull*. Even a Scottish Highland bull doesn't have any eyebrows that you can tell – from the mass of growth on its head that is. Most men of his age have started to trim their eyebrows. His principle idea is to try and compensate for his lack of height. He's always drawing breath, exhales with reluctance, have you spotted it yet? … Knows that it'll affect his stature, you know, makes him look rather like a cock pheasant after it's been rained on.'

It was as if Lauren was a hazardous gas that had to be kept under pressure all day in a steel cylinder, until now, when the valve was opened. I ran my eye up and down one of the columns of dead stags. The mention of the word pheasant made me conscious that I couldn't smell that smell any more – just the odour of ale with the slightest notes of vomit and disinfectant.

'… So, when Patrick says "I'm feeling rather *bullish*", his mind is focussing principally on the animal's *pizzle*. The kind of pizzle he would like others to think that *he* possesses…' I glanced around me to see if anybody was listening.

'Sooner or later he'll be telling you just how many words there are in the French language to describe food and wine, but the chattering heads will tell you that the Lloyd Lewis vocabulary for words to describe the male sexual organ are as numerous as the number of women he's shagged.'

I began to long for a third party. It seemed that there was nothing else for it but to let her flow of garrulous chatter pour over me.

'… Patrick would never use a term like *cock* or *willie*. He believes that through the use of classical terms – and showing respect for his own body – he'll continue to be endowed with a kind of mystical power… Fancy another, hmm?'

The flick-ups of her bobbed hair fell back against her pale neck as she tilted her head back to drain her glass. In spite of the fact I'd barely said a word I was only halfway through mine.

'Yeh… okay…' I rose, held out my hand to take her glass.

'No, I'll get them.' She was on her feet. 'You're the new boy, remember, yes?' I felt even more useless. As she disappeared from view I became aware of the din that was coming from the saloon and lounge. The space around the foot of the stairs had thinned and for a brief moment I had an uninterrupted sight line, through the open front door. The sun had at last made an appearance and I could see it enlivening the back of a red-headed male wearing a sleeveless blue denim trucker. He was standing facing the red-brick wall on the other side of the road, both hands hidden somewhere in front of him. There was an ever-so-faint breeze passing through the house and I could smell a strange but not unpleasant scent of earth and moss which I'd noticed in the butler's pantry that day a month ago. I thought of the canal which ran deep under the hill, the airliner passing in front of the sun, the sparkling tumbler of chilled water, and I was sure that I'd made the right decision. Whether I possessed powers of extra sensory perception or not I would have to wait and see what the Higher Masters held in store for me, if anything.

Lauren seemed to be back in no more than a split second carrying two more glasses of the clear gold-hued liquid. She had the knack of getting served at crowded bars. I didn't.

'Thanks.' I tried hard not to say 'cheers'.

'Phallus yes...' she was still on about Lloyd Lewis's sexual prowess, '... lingam yes, vingle yes, he uses the word member, but Americanisms like womb broom, beaver-basher, Bob Dole, or Little Elvis he'd never utter, hmm. A Spanish-ism such as chorizo might pass muster, but the term Old Man – redolent of an English "musn't grumble" kind of *Daily Mirror*-reading Joe Public of the 1960s is to Patrick the language of the gutter.' She sat back, rested her bob against the moquette upholstery and looked at me, a trace of a smile on her just-slightly-painted lips.

'What about Patrick's marriage? What about Freia?' Her expression switched dramatically, as if I'd just called her a cow.

'How did you know her name?' She pronounced the words as if she was snapping my scale rule over her knee.

'I asked him,' I said with a peffy kind of cough. 'It was clumsy I know.'

'...All before my time.' She said it while exhaling, as if she was calming.

Actually, I knew it wasn't. I'd been asking round, again. The consensus of opinion was that Freia had died about two years ago. I'd also gleaned that Lloyd Lewis had had a succession of administrators, always female, always of a certain social type. None of them had lasted long, and I could see why not, but it appeared that competition for the position was high – fierce in the sense that each of them seemed to have been actively ousted by their successor.

Freia Lloyd Lewis was no secret, she was a name herself in the design world – not as big as His Nibs so, *of course* I knew what her name was. Lauren was being ultra touchy.

'Actually, I have to go.' She drained her glass. I'd barely started my second but I'd no intention of staying on my own. I had an early start tomorrow. She read my thoughts.

'I've a taxi coming in five minutes, where do you live?'

'W4.'

'I'm in Belgravia, I could drop you at Victoria for the District Line, yes.' I had a clear view through the bar and again I caught sight of the blue-denim-clad red-headed man standing with his back to us. Out of the corner of my eye Lauren was a flurry of grey-cotton-clad arms, press-studding leather purse into floppy leather bag concealed within basket-weave holdall. A pug dog of a man wearing black shirt and black silk tie stood in the doorway and raised his arm.

Conversation in the black cab was limited to local geography. As we left the Westway at Shepherd's Bush she smiled again.

'Sorry to give you the bum's rush.' She meant about the beer, I'd obviously overstepped the mark asking about Freia, and she still hadn't forgiven me.

'Sorry not to buy *you* one. I'll get the next,' I said lamely. I opened my wallet to pay my share of the cab.

'Absolutely *not*! It's not every day we have a new office manager starting, but I don't want you to think I get taxis everywhere. Patrick pays me peanuts of *course,* this is trust money for special occasions, yes.'

As the taxi indicated for turning into Terminal Place I leaned forward.

'Actually, can you drop me on Buckingham Palace Road… yeh, here's fine.' I wanted to go into Victoria through the Eccleston Bridge entrance so I could walk back through the new shopping arcade. I also wanted to see which way the taxi went after that.

The taxi paused on the main road and I heard the twitch of the door locks being released. I opened, stepped onto the pavement, and closed behind me. I watched the driver deftly cross into the right lane. The column of traffic was held by a red light. As I walked parallel with the cab I was about to wave but Lauren was looking at something she was holding up in her hand. The light changed and the cab turned right into Eccleston Road in the direction of Eaton Square.

EIGHT

Y ou look familiar.

The head in front of me is resting, tilted back on the train seat headrest... Ears plugged with pearl-like speakers, eyes closed. The hands appear to be at prayer, and between the palms is a silver Walkman.

I'm still trying to place you as the train moves forward, slowly, silently and giving me that curious impression that my carriage is motionless and it's the one on the neighbouring track which is going backwards... Frustrating feeling – illusion of movement, *and* sensation of recognition without context. Like that weird experience of seeing the spitting image of someone you know and being forced to suppress the urge to go up to them and ask, '... do you know Zav Baines by any chance?' Knowing very well that when they say 'No' that you'll have to fight the compulsion to say '... it's just that you look like him so I thought you might know him.' As if... Shit what a blunder! Except this guy doesn't look like anybody I know, I've just seen him before, that's all.

Now I've got you. Hair fashionably short at back and

sides, billowing at the front, like an amber plume of smoke. You've still got the cassette with the Fantin-Latour painting on the cover and you're loading another – the cover a sepia-tinted photo of a youth naked to the waist, shot from above so you can't make out the face... I think it's male although it could be a young woman with very small breasts... except I recognize it now, it's Joe Dallesandro from Andy Warhol's *Flesh*... funny what we remember and what we can't.

You open your eyes, and *there,* you've got me straight away. You speak.

'Going north this time?' You smile, state the obvious. I nod.

'First project... new job.' No harm in saying it.

If I didn't want to talk, this would be the point at which to stop but there's something about you... the two strangers sitting next to us are talking so... 'How about you?'

'... Meeting up with friends – get a flat sorted ready for college start in October...'

'College – doing...?' We appear to be heading for the same city.

'... Spatial Design.'

How weird, 'That's what I did. Do a Foundation course?'

'... Brighton.'

'Of course...' That's what you were doing on the south coast train.

'Enjoy it?'

'Brilliant.'

'Spot-welding, vinyl moulds, spaceframes, grids, permutations, human chess. Lewis Carroll?'

You nod.

'Barcelona trip? Get mugged?'

'And the rest…'

Hilarious, we both laugh.

'Brighton, that's where *I* wanted to go… Had to do mine at the college closest to home – to get the grant, you know.'

'My parents paid the fees,' you say, 'I was fortunate – had free digs with my Auntie. I'm doing the degree course closer to home because my dad's not well. I won't be living at home but I can help out.' I smile.

Funny, you sound like me; no siblings, ill father… Could be what I was fifteen years ago – seeking the bubble reputation. Could be everything I'm not, or what I wanted to be.

I leave you to your music.

NINE

The briefing at GI Group had gone well. I'd been surprised to find that they had a woman CEO… A new broom. I'd rather cheekily asked her opinion on yesterday's first ever space walk by a woman. She replied with a guarded, 'Women are empowering themselves and beginning to fully engage in society…'

Nevertheless, I'd managed to ingratiate myself and we'd decided that out would go the mahogany panelling, the mustard-coloured deep-buttoned chesterfields and in would come an industrial look. We were pondering a glass product called Reglit to achieve maximum daylight throughout the office; all that remained was to check its fireproof credentials. Strange how a company wanting to lose its 'metal-bashing' image was so keen to adopt an industrial one! Patrick would be pleased at my progress.

I left the thirty-seven-storey glass tower block and made my way in the direction of the railway station; up King Street, along Spring Gardens; up Market Street and into the square where I paused for a moment to listen to the racket of starlings in the trees. I stood staring at the be-robed and overblown grubby marble effigy of Queen Victoria spreading her form under a comparatively pint-sized arch. Out of sheer curiosity I ventured to the other side of the monument – which had been ceremoniously daubed with red letters *MUFC* – where there was a further female marble figure also be-robed but bare-breasted and in the act of giving succour to no less than three infants.

''Ellow, Puck, 'ow is you?' The familiar voice seemed to come from nowhere and my heart sank – rather like a block of marble falling into the River Irwell. There was never any point in correcting him with the name thing, he did it with everybody. When I turned, it was to see the same dirty yellow check suit, gold pince-nez, and cigarette ash hair; a mix of game show host and dodgy antiques dealer.

'I'm okay thanks, Mel, how about you?' I tried to disguise the sigh.

'Owe, not three bad.'

Mel Dickson was a mystery, and one I never really wanted to solve. I'd worked with him before – three years previously – here in the north. I'd done a crazy year working for a 'design and build' company, he'd been their senior designer. He was cleverer than he looked. The Cockney patois was ridiculous. Oh, he was from London alright, but rather like an actor forcing himself into character he'd crafted the rhyming slang when he'd moved north.

'... Like the whistle, Mellow.' I winced at my own insincerity, and he peered back through his pince-nez knowing damn well I was bullshitting. '... Still working with Foxton?'

'Nah, 'im brahn bread mate...' Given both of their

social connections I felt it was best not to enquire further. I didn't need to ask.

'It was a Pulman emblem.'

'Really?'

'I knew you was in The Smoke, so what you doing in The Mouth then?

'GI Group, office refurb. What you up to?' I could feel myself adopting his mannerisms.

''Nother club for 'Is Nibs – yer know, Hoodie. Come and have a look.' He'd forgotten the 'butchers'! '…Just dah'n the frog-n-toad…We can ball-n-chalk it from 'ere.' I found myself laughing, he was absurd. He could also be dangerous, I would have to watch my step but I had one advantage, he liked me because he thought I was harmless. I had an hour before my train, and it was on the way so, why not see how the other half lived?

He may have liked me but I can't say I could return the compliment, but though his behaviour occasionally veered towards the sociopathic he at least inhabited the real world; had a wife, two children, and lived in a Barrett house in a respectable suburb. The same did not apply to the man for whom he was working; Mr Hood – *owns 'alf the city if you want to know.'*

Hood lived in a fifteen-bedroom house which stood in twenty-eight acres, and the fact that it was located in one of the wealthy villages outside the city didn't prevent the odd dead body from turning up in the vicinity. Usually an amateur crook he'd had 'pacified'. The police could never pin anything on him, and it was even rumoured that he and the law worked in harmony to maintain a healthy balance in the community.

His victims would often exhibit signs of prehistoric ritual; an eye or finger missing, evidence of sudden – and no doubt involuntary vasectomy, or occasionally discovered Hilti-nailed to the ceilings of deserted factories. I hoped that Hood would not be there.

At six foot three Dickson had developed a stoop, but his strides were massive and I had to trot to keep up. He loped along, Samsonite briefcase dangling from left hand; his varicoloured jacket – which he wore unbuttoned – was swinging in regimental manner, and the rattling coming from his pockets was audible even above the traffic noise.

'Just take a butcher's at the fireman's hose on that,' he motioned with his right hand towards a turbaned man coming towards us. Politically incorrect, downright offensive at times, a part of me couldn't help thinking he was value for money. Dickson's hand formed a salute, the man ignored him, dignified and determined.

A young businessman approached us struggling to consume a hotdog with one hand only, the other on the handle of his briefcase.

'You'll get ghastly writer's enterwrist you will, mate!' Dickson's finger wagged an inch from the frankfurter. The man carried on stolidly.

As we crossed at the station traffic lights a white van was waiting, engine idling, windows down. Inside were two young men with flat-top haircuts, heads nodding to a sound which was like scaffolding falling off the back of a flatbed truck.

Dickson paused, stretched out both arms while holding up his briefcase like an overenthusiastic Chancellor of the Exchequer on budget day, stamped his feet, and wriggled his hips. Shit, he was embarrassing. He was the kind of guy that if you saw him in the street and didn't know him you'd give him a wide berth, but he was like a vaudeville firework and I relished the constant danger of him going off pop.

The club he was designing was in a railway arch beneath the station. We passed through maroon-painted railings the height of three men, clattered our way across granite setts, and headed towards the filthy brick of the railway arches. I followed his yellow check into the mouth of one of the tunnels. There was a roar from above and the hot stink of plumbers welding. To my left I could see a solid door and a dirty yellow-lit window.

He bullied his way through the door, turning the handle but simultaneously kicking it with his mustard-coloured brogue. Inside was the kind of office you associate with all-night taxi services, a sub-human concoction of cork, lino and damp tobacco. Eight-foot strip lights, wood grain laminate on the walls, all sticky to the touch.

'Aiindrea, just the little lady I need to see.' A petite young woman with sculptured blonde quiff was seated at a shiny sapele desk and holding a telephone receiver to her right ear.

'Ellaur Mellaur, lots of porrst ear for Mister 'Ooud. Wants ya to tek it round ta Brazzers as soon as ya can.'

Dickson's grey brows furrowed. ''Ear that, Puck? 'Is Nibs calls.' His voice was low and throaty.

I followed him as he walloped open another door and kicked his way along a dimly lit corridor. He stopped abruptly, as if to sniff the air around him, and groped with his hand against a door on his right, as if he were checking that it was sound. There was a squeak as his hand squeezed the aluminium handle, opened, and poked a light switch on the left-hand wall.

''Is Nibs' office...' he announced, '...one of many... One in each of his establishments if you want to know.' I did. I remembered, though I would perhaps have preferred to have forgotten.

The room into which I followed him was windowless, little more than a cupboard. Behind the door was a grey steel filing cabinet, while opposite the door was a wood and metal desk with three red plastic telephone handsets standing in line. Three piles of mail – each six inches high – had been placed in the centre of the desk. The wall where one might expect a window to be, was covered with a noticeboard crammed with business cards, Post-it notes, and messages scrawled on scraps of lined paper torn from hand-sized pads. Dickson began to rummage.

''Oodie don't like junk.'

I stood in the centre of the room, my eye travelling over the crazy montage on the wall. Some of the stuff must have been there for years... Neat as the desk – and Hood's hatred of junk mail – might be, it was evident that he didn't like to throw things out, inanimate things that is. I was losing interest and about to suggest that I went upstairs and got my train when I was conscious of a pinging sensation in my brain... Not exactly a Eureka moment but something along those lines. On one of the yellow Post-its I could see the word FREIA.

Given that there hadn't been a day over the last month that I hadn't thought about that name it was understandable that I should take a proprietorial interest... None of my business, but before I could help myself my left hand went out and brushed aside the neighbouring note. There it was, handwritten capitals FREIA LLOYD LEWIS, all on one line, nothing else, no message, no number; *nothing*. Dickson saw me stroking the noticeboard.

''Ear, Puck, a *thou* out of place and 'Is Nibs will notice.' His face was dark with warning, '...and it'll be *my* gonads 'e 'as for garters.' I could well imagine that. It felt like a dangerous moment.

'Sorry, Mel, you know me – I'm a curious being.' There was a silence as he fanned the envelopes as if he were shuffling for a round of poker. His lips pursed in an idea.

'Tell you what, Puck. What we are going to do now, is to have a little ride in my jam jar.'

TEN

I knew Mel Dickson well enough to know when he was being melodramatic. My hand movement against the office noticeboard had been quite casual and it was unlikely that it could be interpreted as anything but innocent. Meanwhile, however, a complex psychology had been set in motion. First and foremost, my mind was going quietly bonkers. Bells were clanging, anvils hammering, and pennies were poised waiting to drop. I was hoping that none of them could be seen or heard by anybody but me.

Dickson on the other hand clearly had a different agenda; Mr Hood's mail had to be dealt with, sharpish. There was no time to look at this club.

'You never saw Brazzers did you?' He caught me looking at my watch. I had two choices, i) to walk upstairs and get my return train to London which would be leaving in twelve minutes, or, ii) get into Dickson's car and let him drive me for the ten minutes it would take to get to Brazzers; ten minutes looking at the club, ten back and I would get the next train. It was no contest, my mind *had* to have more information '...one of many, one in each of his establishments if you want to know'.

I followed Dickson back out of the dankness of the railway arch. He turned left, going deeper into the Victorian catacombs that ran under the railway station. My feet tapped across granite setts, crunched across a floor of cinders to where a ghostly pale blue metallic saloon was parked diagonally. With its long bonnet it seemed like a beacon of hi-tech modernity set against the Piranesi world of charred and leprous brick.

'... Still got the Starship Enterprise then, Mel?'

'Owe you mean the Sitter-on... Never leave 'owme without it,' he tapped the side of his nose twice... I knew, it was incongruous that a man who styled himself as an antiques game show host should drive something like this, but Mel Dickson was a tangle of contradictions.

'Hydro-pneumatic integral self-levelling suspension; remember, Puck?' I did – only too well.

His right hand touched the ignition, on went the headlamps and I witnessed the spectre of the car bonnet rising and the lamp beams hitting the brick walls. Down here, beneath the railway station it was a world of darkness lit only by the lights of Dickson's car. All was monochrome; it reminded me of the moon landings.

Outside the station Dickson headed east. He was driving fast and menacing nice people in Morris Minors. We tore past a slim girl on the pavement wearing white flared trousers.

'Jeezus, look at the Lionel Blairs on that!' He was driving like hell, down street after street of desperate pink terraces, past high walls which looked as though they encircled prisons. Through a wasteland of demolished buildings, past factories with castle-like towers, under cranes, towards smoking fires. I could see the moors in the distance and I felt a sudden need to go to the lavatory.

Abruptly he veered left and I heard/felt the tearing of coke cinders under car tyres – heard the ratchetting of the handbrake.

Outside looked like a disused coalmine pithead. There was a tall rusted steel frame with a giant wheel, rows of lock-up containers, scratched, decayed and diseased. The building he had parked next to was eight storeys of black brick, punctured at regular intervals with windows. It had a tower which rose grimly into the air like a Schloss Lichtenstein. The car bonnet sank slowly like an oversized metallic cushion deflating itself.

'Brazzers!' He pursed in apparent satisfaction, nodding like a proud dad watching his daughter perform in the school play. He eased himself out of the driver's seat fanning the wad of post in his right hand while his left slammed the door. The central locking system made that little sucking sound. This time the Samsonite briefcase stayed on the back seat of the car.

'Follow,' he grunted. I did so down a flight of calcined stone steps, along a subterranean corridor of saliva-coloured glazed brick. Perhaps there was a toilet here.

He yanked open a steel-panelled door. Inside there were people… a kind of office, desks, cork noticeboards, and paper – wads of it. Like the one at the Station Club it was lined with wood grain formica, at least it felt normal.

There was a girl sitting at a sapele desk, bottle-red quiff – shiny green fat-shouldered jacket.

'Do you have a toilet I can use?' As I headed for the *jakes* I could see Dickson out of the corner of my eye, on tiptoe, competing for height with the girl's big hair. He looked like an artful schoolboy his hands behind him concealing the fan of letters.

I felt better after a pee.

'No time for pointing Percy, Puck, come!' I followed to where I could smell wet plaster, my shoes were sticking to lino, and I could see Dickson hovering in front of me in the glare of the fluorescent, his hand doing the smoothing ritual, this time with a drippy-painted grey door. His fingers closed over the handle and pushed it open. As he did so I noticed that although the door was unlocked it had a keyhole.

Inside it was a dismal replica of the place we'd been in less than fifteen minutes previously. Dickson began arranging envelopes on top of the desk like an obedient child playing patience with oversized cards. Feeling almost sick with excitement I moved across the room to the noticeboard, my eye flitting backwards and forwards between the mass of names, messages and memorabilia and Dickson's hunched head and shoulders. Every so often I caught him eyeing me over the top of his pince-nez. It was like playing Stare-Stare.

At last I saw it. I knew it would be there. Even so, when I did I nearly jumped out of my skin; FREIA LLOYD LEWIS 01-2... the last six digits were obscured by a photograph of a black jazz saxophonist. The photograph was fixed to the noticeboard with white mapping pins – but only at the top. Trying to appear as casual as possible I lifted the bottom of the photograph with my thumb and finger.

'Come on, Puck. Mr Hood calls!' I had no more than a fleeting glimpse of the number. Insufficient to commit it to my muddled memory. I let the photo drop back against the notice board. There was nothing I could do, no trick, nothing – too risky. I turned and followed Dickson out of the room.

Was it all a coincidence, was I getting myself into a tizzy over nothing? My head was asking the questions but my viscera were giving the answers. There were three possibilities; i) it was a different Freia Lloyd Lewis, ii) she was either an acquaintance – or had done business with Hood, iii) behind the name and number had been a plan of intent by a third party, and it was this last alternative which was gripping me… A plan of intent, involving criminal offence? Come on, Pulse! Nobody would be mad enough to leave evidence like this.

But Hood wasn't 'nobody', nor was he normal. *'One of many, one in each of his establishments if you want to know.'* The noticeboards were 'show and tell', they were trophy cabinets, they were his twisted *curriculum vitae*, his warped showreel. If the law ever made it as far as one of these dens it would be, 'yes Mr Hood, no Mr Hood, and thank you for the information, Mr Hood.' The chain of command would be long, stretching so far away from Hood that it would always be easy for him to sever its last few links.

I followed Dickson through cave-like spaces. At first the rooms were tall and of white-painted brick, but soon we were passing through low chambers of raw rough render and galvanized steel where the smell of drying mortar became more intense. I could see moving lights ahead of me and the air seemed warmer. There was that resounding echoing feel that you get when you're crossing from a small space into a very large volume, and all at once everything felt huge as if I'd suddenly dropped into a giant sinkhole.

Dickson was standing in front of me so my view straight ahead was blocked. On either side of me stretched rows of small tables and chairs, hundreds of them. There were those bloody awful gig lamps he'd always used in schemes, and fake candles on the tables. There were woody-looking alcoves with upholstered banquette seating, shelves of phoney books… and stuffed owls… his idea of sophistication.

On the edges of the giant circle in which I was standing I could see the twinkle of three bars; slicker, shinier, black and red with lots of chrome. Dickson stepped sideways and made a gesture as if he was inviting me to step on stage. I had a proper view now, straight down across the dance floor. It was massive. You could get two thousand people on it. Xenon? … Nothing like this. Stringfellows? … Tiny. The Hacienda? … Pokey. This was Roman, an amphitheatre. It was bread and circuses.

Overhead was a steel spider's web of lights, gantries, and rigs. Lacelike non-structures and patterns of light and shadow were slowly wheeling across the smooth gunmetal floor. I was aware that the whole dance floor was slowly rotating, moving clockwise, while the DJ console was leisurely travelling the opposite way.

"'Ellow, Mellobydick, how is you?'

I could see where the voice was coming from, a man standing in the centre of the console. He'd had his back towards us until now, but as the console rotated a face came into view. The head, backlit by one of the overhead spotlights, seemed to generate an aura of evil.

I'd met Hood once before but I hadn't forgotten. The long head with its oddly cherubic appearance, like that of Henry Spencer in the film *Eraserhead*. Hair cropped back

and sides rising darkly from the crown. Features childish –
the eyes unruly like the police mugshot of Brady taken less
than eight hours after he'd killed.

I followed Dickson onto the dance floor and came to a
stop three metres from Hood. I could see the scar running
vertically from his upper lip, over his chin, and sliding in
and out of the dimple. The dimple was the only human
thing about him.

'Owe not three bad,' mumbled Dickson in a grovelly
sort of way.

'What doing? Who am brought us you this time?'
The slit of the mouth widened in recognition. 'We-ell, Mr
Puckeroon!'

'Puck and me bumped into one another in town.' It
sounded like he'd been caught in the act of something and
was making excuses.

'… Hope that didn't hurt, Mellobydick.'

'… Not at all, Mr Hood… Puck working here on
project.'

'What projay am this, Mr Puckeroon?'

'GI Group.' I didn't feel like giving details.

'My mother knew a lot of GIs in the war… Am like.'

I'd forgotten how weird the accent was; Northern
Irish, Canadian, New Zealand? It was as if he'd spent his
formative years in a cluster of British colonies. The bizarre
word arrangements weren't dialect, they were Hoodspeak.

''Ellow, Stripy!'

A huge cat wandered out from behind the console. I
expected Hood to kick it, but instead he walked towards
it. One step with his right leg while dragging his left leg
behind him. He bent down and picked up the creature with

a disconcerting gentleness, right hand gripping the front of the feline body, his left smoothing its rear end. He stood there with the giant furry bundle in his arms. The cat's head was as big as his.

'... Siamese.' Hood's head nodded down at the cat's head.

What? Pull the other one! This was an oversized nightclub-inhabiting moggie if ever I saw one. He read my thoughts.

'... Separated from her sister, shortly after birth,' he insisted. A faint bell rang in my head – not a full-on carillon, more a distant angelus.

'We nem GI Group, doesn't we, Mellobydick?' Dickson stared at the shiny grey floor.

'... Lots of post for you, Mr Hood. On desk... In office... if that's all, Mr Hood...?' Dickson began walking backwards the way we'd come, he looked frightened to turn, as if he expected to be transformed into a pillar of salt.

'Don't do anything I wouldn't do, Mr Puckeroon!'

As I followed Dickson back over the dance floor in the direction of the door I heard the almost inaudible mutter.

'Those GIs were really something.'

As a subdued Dickson drove me back to the railway station I made a silent resolution. There was nothing else for it. I had to come back and get that telephone number, on my own, and soon.

ELEVEN

'Lauren's gone to the bank. Slip upstairs to my apartment, Pulse, and bring me the key…'

I was standing in Patrick's office. He was sitting behind his walnut leviathan. He hadn't even looked up from the pages of *The Times* which lay open, flat, and almost certainly ironed by Lauren who had been here since very early.

'How did you get on in the city of eternal rain?' He spoke the words as if he'd just awoken from a year-long sleep. He also sounded smug, it was warm and sunny outside, he'd got both of the floor-length sash windows open at the bottom and I could feel a breeze against my leg. A trio of bees was interesting itself in the honeysuckle grown in pots against the trellis of the neighbouring house. I'd gathered that Patrick hated clutter and that included the balcony. There was no sign of the huge mackerel cat.

'Very well actually, I…'

'I suppose you're going to tell me how picturesque terracotta looks when it's wet.'

'Very good actually…'

'… It's to open the third drawer in my desk, here.' At last he looked up. I'd almost forgotten what he was asking me to do.

'The keys to the flat are kept in the top drawer which is *always* open.' I stared at him. Why couldn't he do it himself, or wait till Lauren got back?

There was a rich woodwind sound as he pulled open the top drawer, took out two keys, and held them up in front of him as if he were a pope holding the tip of his paterissa.

'It's kept in the steel wall cabinet in the kitchen, third from the right – top row. It's hollow, antique, like the desk.' I was already starting to lose track.

'In order to open the steel wall cabinet, you'll need another key. That's kept in the knife drawer which is to the left of the hob top.' He pointed the keys at me and I took them.

'Should I knock?'

'Why?'

'… I thought Martinique might be there.' He looked at me as if I was a child who'd asked him something very simple such as '*why do you wear a tie?*'

'You don't seem to know a lot about women.' I could feel myself blushing. 'Have you got children?' He said it as if he was throwing something at me.

'No.'

'*I've* got three. Take your time.' He made it sound almost provocative. '…Have a look at the roof garden,' he purred.

I left the room in a mixture of uncertainty and embarrassment. Perhaps that's what he wanted… Me the intruder, him sitting downstairs visualizing my every movement while he pretended to read *The Times*. Perhaps the answer lay in the roof garden.

I tapped my way up the two remaining flights of steps and stopped outside the door which led to the flat. It felt unsatisfactory coming to a stop like that, a blank white wall, a black-painted door. In a house like this I would have expected more ceremony. In the days before the apartment existed there would have been an open landing with three bedrooms and from that a narrow stair leading up to three further loft bedrooms. A five-storey house like this would have had at least two live-in servants and they wouldn't have had a room each.

I had the two keys in my hand; a Yale, and a Chubb. I tried the Chubb; the mechanism rolled over – satisfying, almost noiseless like a gear change in the hand of a competent driver. I could imagine the moistness of the oil in its internal works. Nobody was at home, I could feel it. I turned the Yale, pushed the door with my right hand. The sensation was like lifting the top of an exquisitely-made jewellery box; soft, silent, a close fit. There was a scent of vanilla and for the second time I forgot about the rotten pheasant niff from below.

Inside, the floor was covered with carpet the colour and texture of peach skin. There was little similarity with the weird world of below. It seemed normal; a normal domain for normal people, neat, tasteful, ordered – even slightly dull. There was still a white wall regime, but not totalitarian, and here and there was even a hint of taupe. The paintings and drawings had a more human quality; street scenes in black ink, traditional watercolours, still lifes. All the doors in the flat were standing open exactly one foot.

The storey where I was standing was made up entirely of bedrooms; one single, one guest double with en suite, a family bathroom, and the master with en suite. As I peered round one of the doors I could see that furniture was fitted and all puzzlingly pale – it was difficult to see what was wardrobe and what was wall. There were no hand-tooled leather headboards, no lascivious carvings.

I padded upstairs where I found a similar narrative of calm... A further bedroom – a single this time with a separate shower and WC. Perhaps all these rooms would be in use when the three children were here, and Lauren had said that Martinique's son visited a lot... Maybe he slept on the sofa – unless two of the children shared the guest room. One of the children was married wasn't she... did the husband ever stay, and if so where did the menu-wielding two-year-old take its rest?

There was a separate sitting room at the front of the house whose door, like the others, stood open just far enough for me to see that part of its ceiling followed the line of the sloping roof. The rest of the apartment was open-plan; a kitchen facing outboard, and a dining area – inboard, but directly under a large light cannon, and adjacent to a set of French doors leading out onto a roof terrace. I put my hand on the backrest of one of the eight black Eames dining chairs arranged around the white-topped dining table. There was no sunlight falling directly onto the table but the interior space seemed to be full of brightness. By midday it would be like a hothouse but then I noticed – just under the lip of the light cannon – the protruding edge of a power-operated *brise soleil*. It was clever, a space which spoke of well-defined activities but without ostentation... A world away from the abandoned garden and the *Parsifal* bench below.

I clicked open the steel-framed French door and stepped onto the white terrazzo-paved terrace. The inboard wall was white-painted render, the party wall rendered in fair-faced sand and cement. Against the white wall stood a circular table surrounded by six white Panton chairs. At the centre of the white table was a wooden tray – made from chunky pieces of teak half-housed so it looked like a giant waffle with a thick rim. The rear parapet wall had been removed and replaced with white-painted horizontal railings of the type seen on ocean liners of the 1930s, and giving an uninterrupted view north. In the morning sun the treetops seemed to have acquired the illuminance of fool's gold.

I closed the French doors, crossed the dining area and, as I looked upward through the light cannon, I could see the tiny profile of an airliner. Simultaneously there was a stroboscopic flicker coming through the open door of the sitting room as the plane passed in front of the sun. I thought of the inspection chamber fifty feet below me, and a hundred feet below that the canal.

I crossed to the knife drawer, opened, and took out the key for the steel cupboard. I removed the knobbly desk key, locked cupboard, replaced key in knife drawer, walked downstairs, pulled the apartment door closed behind me, turned the Chubb, and tapped my way back down to Patrick's office. The whole operation had taken precisely seven minutes. I handed him the knobbly key, he took it, closed his fist around it and looked at me as if he were about to accuse me of something.

'I'm hosting supper,' he said it as if he were announcing his intention to preside over mass at St Peter's in Rome. '…on Saturday. I hope you will come,' he whispered.

'Er… my friend's coming for the weekend; we were hoping to have dinner somewhere.' The eyes fixed me, black with what seemed to me a combination of curiosity and fury.

'Per-haps you *and* your friend can come. My children will be here, and…' he sniffed hard and pouted with his upper lip, '… Martinique's son.' The trace of a smile – not kindly – appeared on his face.

'What!… is your *friend's* name?' As he emphasized the '*friend*' his nose seemed flatter, his neck goiterous, as if it had been injected with pure suspicion.

'Denise.'

'French names do *so* become a woman I think, don't you?' The fury abruptly evaporated, the nose seemed fleshier, the neck more relaxed. The curiosity remained and was joined by apparent celebration in the form of the 'O' sound and the motion of his lips. The dock-leaf leather under his backside squeaked appreciatively.

'… Seven o'clock.'

It was not clear whether or not it would be a joint effort with Martinique, no mention of her name had been made other than the curt reference to her son.

TWELVE

Denise and I had talked for quite a time about what we should take to Patrick's supper event. Wine was out of the question after what Lauren had told me; home-made chutney? Home-made *anything* could end up having gallons of scorn poured over it if Patrick had anything to do with it. In the end we settled for 160-gram Traditional Shortbread Fingers from Fortnum and Mason. It was after all only a token.

Denise and I weren't really an item. I'd known her for years and the relationship was what some people might – and inaccurately so – refer to as 'off and on'. We saw one another anywhere between a few times a year and once every few years. She was a maverick... Failed to complete her degree because – by her own admission – she was busy having at least one abortion, finally giving birth to a son who, evidently, was fortunate to have survived. She too had only just come through the ordeal but in doing so had an out-of-body experience.

Her revelation held me in a state of awe and inadequacy. I was receptive to the notion of paranormal happenings but doubtful that they would ever happen to me. But more so because as a man I knew that I would never undergo either an abortion or a near-death experience as a result of childbirth. 'Living *real* life', she called it.

It wasn't as brutal as it sounded to say that, as a painter, she was talentless. She'd never properly tapped into the creative side of her personality. She was an accomplished cook, but more interestingly an incontinent collector of husbands having recently divorced number three, and to both of our credits in the adultery stakes we had only ever *liaised* in the periods between husbands. 'I'm between husbands,' she would say – '… resting dahling, but it's not much of a rest!'

'Why *don't* you get married?' she was always saying to me.

'Why *do* you get married?' I would reply.

Denise's talent in life was in finding folk to fill the gaps in her own, and like a conductor brings in the right instruments at the right time she seemed to do it with people.

I'd never hung out with her at college because she would have thought I was a swot, while she was living her authentic sensual life. Dad was a high-grade civil servant… mum ran a smallholding; pigs, cows, sheep – so Denise grew up a country girl, and that's exactly what she looked like; round-headed, apple-cheeked, rabbity hair so soft it wouldn't do anything, and after she'd stayed the night at my place I would find hair pins everywhere.

She worked in advertising for a couple of companies, didn't like being told what to do, found an admiring middle-aged businessman who believed she could bring in work, turn it round, make a profit. They were right, she did, and I admired her for it. It seemed to me that somewhere here was a parallel – well a kind of mirror in that Patrick was setting me up in business. He'd get the work in, I'd turn it round. Everything was there for me, it was just up to me, if I was up to it.

I thought I'd give Denise a quiet tour round the ground floor and basement before we went up to the apartment.

'You're getting better,' she exclaimed as she peered round my drawing board and stared unseeingly at a floor plan of GI Group.

'Ahem!' There was a creak of leather brogue by the open studio door. He must have been in the basement while the two of us let ourselves in at the front door.

'Patrick Lloyd Lewis, *(Conservative)*' he advanced towards Denise his hand aiming for hers. He took it, broad thumb pressing down on her fingers while his four square digits played with their underside. He leaned forward, brought her hand to his 'O' shaped lips, and still holding her hand…

'I've heard *so* much about you.' He hadn't. Denise's top lip puckered, then she broke into one of her deep throaty chuckles. I'd never figured out whether this liberated laughter was a sign of mateyness, woman-of-the-worldishness, or proof of a deep understanding of human nature. Whichever it was, it *was* Denise, and when it happened in restaurants, which was often, I was always aware of the furrowings which appeared on the foreheads of nearby diners.

His lips were still nuzzling her fingers when he turned his face to me.

'You've been keeping her very close to your chest.' It was delivered in exactly the same tone as '*I've been having a few moments with my late wife.'* I was amused at his skilful self-contradiction and laughed. I noticed the pinkness of his ear and recalled that gentle brush from the back of Martinique's fingers she'd given his shoulder during my interview.

Denise laughed also, this time less throatily, and without warning the 'O' shape of the lips took on the dark fissured texture of the anus of some unknown creature.

'Come!' he bellowed as if he'd had enough of all that. We followed, out of the studio; Patrick, Denise, and me as vanguard walking up the four flights of stone steps. Patrick was dressed in navy blazer, grey worsteds, but his tie had undergone yet another minute change. Its stripes ran horizontally instead of the usual diagonal.

'You have to be fit to live here!' I commented lamely as he opened the apartment door. The aroma of vanilla was still there but was overlaid with something dark, animalistic, but nevertheless appetizing.

'Oooh, but I am.' Patrick's reply was followed by another catarrh-driven chuckle from Denise. I arrived at the top of the final stair in time to see Martinique with a metal ladle in her hand and wearing a navy and white striped apron which reached to her mid calf. On her head was a white chef's hat – not a tall toque, just a short one. Her complexion had acquired the shine and hue of olive oil.

'Martiniqua! Look who *I've* brought,' he announced. It was two minutes past seven. I got the feeling we were early.

'Hellowe,'

'Helloo.'

'Hello.'

'I know I *look* like the chef but I'm not… Not even a *sous* – more a kitchen porter…' She pulled the hat from her head and tossed her bobbed hair into shape. Again, it struck me how similar were the styles of her and Lauren. But it proved the point that making people wear a uniform doesn't make them all look the same. Lauren walked with her head forward, hair like a helmet – a soft one swishing from left to right. She would never shake *her* head in such a carefree manner.

'It's Laurie's meal really; he's gone to fetch his knives.'

I had a mental picture involving fire-eating and knife-throwing, but Martinique explained that Laurie was in London doing a catering course. 'I hope you like beef.' Denise and I nodded but Denise looked surprised. Martinique seemed to read her thought.

'It's Sunday lunch really – transposed to Saturday evening. Lunchtime is too early to expect all the family to get here, and we've got another celebration tomorrow evening.' I heard Patrick inhaling grandly as he left the room. I was looking forward to meeting Laurie.

I sneaked the shortbread onto a nearby shelf while Denise assured Martinique that one of her three brothers had done a catering course, and was now professor of philosophy at Arcadia Uni, Ohio. I wondered whether the two of them would get on, after all, they both had sons of about the same age.

'I imagine that Patrick's gone down to find you something to drink.' I'd heard the flat door opening and the tap-tap of his brogues on the stone stairs. I wondered where his cellar was and thought of the canal running all that distance beneath our feet.

'You can sit here – anywhere for now but we may rearrange you later… or perhaps out on the terrace?' It was agreeably warm, and there were long shadows but…

'We'd quite like to be here, where the action is.' I glanced at Denise who obviously agreed with me. Her eyes had a look as if my remark might well be prophetic. Denise sat at the end of the window-side of the table, which was laid for eight; I placed myself opposite and assumed that Patrick would take that head of the table, Martinique the other end.

'You won't have had this one before!' Patrick glided back through the door carrying two galvanised aluminium buckets. I hadn't heard him close the apartment door.

One bucket was half-full of ice and contained four bottles; the other iceless pail had six bottles protruding at various angles like glass skittles. He plucked one of the non-chilled vessels and gently cradled it in front of the two of us like a father parading his newborn. The label had the feel of a circus poster of the Edwardian era.

Martinique untied her apron, whipped off the hat again, hung both on a steel peg by the hob top and darted out of the room.

'Ahl-low!' The voice coming from below was a parody of 'Mr Angry' a character I'd heard on a Radio 1 phone-in programme. Male or female? ...Wasn't possible to tell, so when the figure entered I didn't feel surprised either way. What *did* take me aback was the similarity in look to Patrick. The person who bowled into the room was female, early twenties, five foot seven, stocky, broad-chinned, flat-nosed, but instead of the black pupils she had the most wonderful pale bright blue sparkly eyes which seemed ever so familiar.

'*"You won't have had this one before..."* Has he said that yet?' Her parody of Patrick sounded a little breathless. I nodded to the newcomer like an obedient dog. 'That's because it's from his very own vineyard,' she added. Patrick pursed his lips, stood on tiptoe. This I took to be a kind of double pride; acknowledgement of his oenological achievement plus the fact that the information was coming from a chip off his own block.

'Really?' I couldn't think of anything else to say. The newcomer sat down next to Denise. Patrick meanwhile was conspicuously corkscrewing the non-iced bottles.

'Martiniqua, glasses!' As if on cue Martinique hurried into the room dressed like a matelot in hooped top and white trousers. Her skin was less shiny than it had been at her exit. More obvious than ever were the differences between her and Lauren, and also her ability to fit in. If you saw Martinique walking down Whitehall she would look like most power-dressed female Brits, but if you caught sight of her sauntering along a street in Toulouse you wouldn't consider that she was anything but native French. On the other hand, if Lauren was beamed down to the Toulouse street she would stick out like a sore Brit.

I stared at the 'ahl-low' female. She raised both eyebrows and smiled without showing her teeth. She was dressed in a voluminous green – almost *dayglo* – smock and blue denim jeans.

'Yippee I oh ki yay!' The voice coming from below was not dissimilar to the one of thirty seconds previously except this time it was discernibly female. I found myself standing – partly out of politeness, but mainly through astonishment – because the person who burst through the door, surely, was the she who was sitting almost opposite me? They were twins – same smock, same jeans.

'Bea-Bea!'

'Jen-Jen!' There was noisy air-kissing and the space under the roof light seemed to be a tangle of hazard green.

'How was Argentina?'

I'd got my bearings now. It was Bea who was sitting opposite me. I knew about Jen because she was the mother of the two-year-old amateur eye surgeon… And so, it unrolled that Bea was a journalist currently working on a piece called *Falklands Fallout*.

'We both trained as architects then I went and did something different,' announced Bea to no one in particular. Introductions it seemed were not the thing here.

'Yo yo!' The voice from below was unequivocally male, and as the young man came in I could see he was a few years younger than the girls… About my height – five ten – he hesitated at the other end of the table before taking a seat next to Jen. Martinique walked round the table placing a number of small white bowls across its surface containing fat olives, giant cashews, and plain crisps the size of small papadums. The girls each took a crisp and munched with mouths tightly closed. There was the sound of a cork popping followed by a soft fizzing, and on her second circuit Martinique handed each person a wine glass containing an aerated light golden liquid.

'It's a new one. I'm interested to hear what you all think.' Patrick's lips were in the 'O' shape, his head tilted and turned like a small girl who's just finished reading her poem to the class.

'Cheers, Dad.' Al downed it in one. Patrick was standing behind me and I realized he was waiting for my comment.

'Very nice, Patrick…'

I felt his eye travelling down my back.

'Did you know that your mother dropped a stitch when she knitted your pullover?'

Because the evening temperatures were down to 12^0 or less, I'd worn a sleeveless Fair Isle under my jacket. They were enjoying a fashion revival so I'd sported it with a grey tab-collar shirt, buttoned but no tie. I thought it looked quite good. I knew all about the dropped stitch in the middle of the back and had never had the heart to tell my mother. As I usually wore it with a jacket it had never seemed to matter but this evening was warm – even with the French windows standing open – and I'd removed my jacket. Patrick was still wearing his. He turned to Denise who seemed to be about to offer her verdict of the wine.

'If it isn't Blanquette de Limoux it's a blend using that as a base, *methode traditionelle...*' Denise raised her glass and turned it, '... Probably Languedoc region.'

Patrick moved away from my back, round the end of the table, and practically fell on his knees in front of her.

'You and I have something to talk about. *Don't* go away.'

'This would be very good drunk with oysters,' insisted Denise.

'Do you eat oysters often?' asked Patrick, the irises of his eyes bigger and blacker than I had ever seen them before.

'Oooh yes,' Denise let out another of her throaty chuckles. I knew she did, unlike me she was an experienced and accomplished cook. *Are they fresh?* She would always interrogate the red-faced fishmonger, a question which to my inexperienced ears seemed superfluous. If they weren't fresh then why were they on his stall? And if the monger was unscrupulous enough to be offering produce which wasn't fresh then surely, he wouldn't admit to it anyway?

Shortly after one of the '*are they fresh*' incidents I happened to see a TV programme on oysters, and with my new-found knowledge I rather swottishly suggested to Denise that a more pertinent question might be *are they 'rock' or 'native'*? She hadn't heard of either.

Patrick marched to the knife drawer, took out a carving knife and – what looked to me – like a large screwdriver. He planted the steel in the centre of the butcher's block with his left hand and began vigorously drawing the flat of the knife across it, first one side then the other. Conversation among the three children buzzed. Denise let out another of her throaty chuckles.

'We were just saying, Al, isn't it funny that all three of us did architecture? I dropped out after three years; Jen was the only one to qualify…' Bea was addressing her siblings but the story was clearly for Denise and my benefit.

'I needed something home-based for the babe.'

'… and Al flunked after a year.'

'… Didn't suit me.'

'It was living in a house with all those girls that did it – where else would you have got the idea of changing courses and doing fashion?'

At first, I thought Jen was referring to Al being the only son – and 'all those girls' being the family home – but clearly all three children had their own flats, lived their own lives. Al was silent. There was the sound of oven doors being opened and closed. I could see Martinique prodding things. The smell was more appetizing than ever – my taste buds had been stimulated by the sparkling wine.

Had I encountered Bea or Jen on separate occasions I would have assumed that they were the same person. Patrick had referred to his trio of offspring as 'my children' – no names. As far as I was concerned Bea and Jen looked like mirror images and it was only through sitting next to one and opposite the other that I began to see them as two individuals.

Both had similar light brown hair; touches of blonde and henna – Bea more *Bananarama* flyaway, Jen a neater – like the girl dancers in the *Human League* – longer-style Eton Crop. They both had the startling blue eyes which I'd seen somewhere before, both formed 'O's with their lips, and both regularly engaged in the backward tilt of their heads as if they were examining a set of cross-hair sights located on the end of their noses. But if anyone looked like Patrick it was Bea; the flat nose, the thick neck, and as she indulged in one of her backward tilts to the head I was sure I could make out the trace of an Adam's apple. Jen's features were smaller, neater – more feminine.

'Hi everyone!' A tall young man appeared in the room dressed in black trousers and white shirt. He crossed the room towards Denise and me.

'Hello, I'm Laurie, you must be Denise, and you must be Pulse.' I was amazed. Not only was he the first person in the room to offer a greeting, for a seventeen-year-old he seemed remarkably mature. Tall – taller than me, but he didn't have that hulking gaucheness that a lot of oversized teens have – as if they were unformed humans teetering on the edge of catastrophe. He had the aura of a man of thirty, and his English was immaculate. He was carrying a small wooden case with a handle.

'I've got a boy *just* his age,' Denise turned to Bea as Laurie walked away. Bea turned to Jen and the two of them exchanged deadpan looks breathing in unison through their noses.

Laurie walked over to the butcher's block where Patrick was still thrashing the carving knife against the steel. There was a brief exchange between Patrick and Martinique which I could just hear over the talking hive of the three siblings. Denise had managed to start something – if somewhat perfunctory – with Bea... about Argentina.

'Laurie wants to carve the beef, Patrick.'

'I'm perfectly capable of carving my own joint of beef...' he continued lacerating at the steel '... which *I* paid for.'

'It's what he's been doing today, he wants to practise – there's no need for you to do that, Patrick, he's brought his own knives.'

'So, *my* knife isn't good enough.' His foot stamped down on the tiled floor.

'It's not that, Patrick; it's what he's been learning on his course.'

I was abruptly aware of the scuffling of leather against the marble floor. I felt a rush of wind behind my back, and saw Patrick marching past his empty chair towards the French window. He was holding the carving knife – holding it like a dagger. The scene had endowed itself with the bizarre appearance of a non-costume rehearsal for Macbeth. I heard the slam of the French door followed by an almighty thump. Denise closed her eyes, while the three siblings carried on chattering.

Laurie was already carving the beef, Martinique removing various vegetables from the oven and saucepan and transferring them into tureens. I could hear the crash of dinner plates. As Denise moved her head in an attempt to join Bea's chatter I had a view through the French doors onto the terrace. It appeared to be deserted, and I could see the circular white table upon which lay the wooden waffle-shaped tray. Something was protruding vertically from the chunky teak. It was still quivering slightly.

'I'm serving out directly onto plates – cafeteria style,' instructed Laurie.

'No beef for me,' from Al.

'Al's a veggie...' Jen spoke directly to Denise and me for the first time, '... he's done it just to spite Dad.'

'The English eat far too much *rosbif.*' Laurie's exaggerated Franglais sounded odd next to his perfect English.

A bovine roar rose up from out on the roof terrace.

'If I haven't been sufficiently generous then please help yourselves.' Martinique transferred the lidded tureens onto the table, and Laurie distributed the plates now loaded with a delicious-looking combination of meat and vegetables. Martinique put out fresh wine glasses, polishing each one as she placed it on the table.

On my plate – in addition to the thinnest slices of beef I'd ever seen – were three small new potatoes, two larger roast potatoes, julienned carrots and parsnips – also roast – and four perfectly aligned stalks of asparagus. As I helped myself to what appeared to be horseradish I heard the click of the French door and once again was aware of Patrick hurrying past me, this time making less noise. He took one of the bottles with the Edwardian circus-type label and did the entire circuit of the table filling each person's glass with the dark red wine.

I couldn't help contrasting in my mind this scene with that of Sunday lunches at home with Mum and Dad. Chops were the rule with no more than a cubic inch of lean on each. Spuds were painstakingly peeled in a bowl by Dad while he watched football in flickering black and white. To save time my mother would resort to tinned vegetables, and she had never been a great one for spotted dick, suet or treacle puds, so 'afters' would usually follow the 1960s convenience formula of Instant Whip, or if my mother's fourteen-stone sister was expected, a lemon Royal Chiffon. The only time we had a joint of meat was when we had a visitor, and Dad would attempt to carve whilst breathing heavily and making a great deal of clattering.

'I can't wait for your verdicts.' Patrick's voice sounded oddly low and flat. I gathered that this vintage was his. Al took a manly slurp.

'Not bad, Dad.' Patrick certainly wouldn't be asking for my opinion again but I knew who he *would* be asking. As he took his seat at the head of the table Denise took a sip, bent forward and whispered something to him. I couldn't help noticing that in reply Patrick's right hand disappeared somewhere under the table. Denise gave a throaty chuckle. I saw Martinique glance their way, her eyes in conference mode.

I cut some beef, skewered a new potato with my fork and raised it to my mouth. Patrick was watching me. 'What did you think of Wimbledon, Pulse?' His voice seemed unnaturally loud, and there was a silence as I chewed and swallowed conspicuously with the feeling that everyone was awaiting my response. Evidently Patrick, Martinique and the three siblings had been. All had had tickets for Centre Court. I hadn't even watched it on TV. He persisted.

'... Lords?' I wasn't sure whether he meant The House

or cricket. 'I know you live in W4, don't tell me, you're a closet Brentford fan?' He pursed his lips.

'Dad's only showing off because he gets VIP tickets for Arsenal,' said Jen – rather a spirited defence of me I thought – '… from Uncle Falco,' she added.

'Yes, the two of them park the Jenson somewhere discreet and eat fish and chips out of a polystyrene container,' echoed Bea. Patrick leaned back in his Eames chair as if taking applause for this endorsement of him as a man of the people.

'Is there *any* sport that you like, Pulse?'

'Swimming…'

'I see.'

'I went to Glyndebourne,' offered Denise.

Patrick's lips formed the 'O'.

'I thought the arias weren't as good as last year,' said Jen.

'The soprano was weak,' insisted Bea.

'Actually, it was last year I went. The season hasn't started this year,' reminded Denise who smiled at Patrick, and held up her glass. 'I always think wines are better when the grapes are not over-blended,' continued Denise. I noticed Patrick's bottom lip moving as if his tongue was pushing against it. 'Blending more than three grapes at a time is a bit like an artist mixing too many colours on his palette. He has this misguided notion that because red, green and blue are so delicious-looking that if he mixes them together it will produce a super colour, and what does he get? … Mud.'

Patrick's eyes had become blacker than coal and the skin around his mouth had puckered like the anus of some unknown creature.

'I've never seen anyone eat asparagus like that before.' Patrick was looking at me sideways and forcing his lips into a smile, as if he were an indulgent father watching his child struggle to express itself in some perverse way. I'd started to eat the asparagus from the 'big end' where the stalks were at their widest – saving the most tender and best for last.

'I must confess that the only asparagus I've eaten before has been in liquidised form, courtesy of Messrs Heinz.' Everybody laughed – perhaps at my honesty. It was by no means the first time I'd wanted to tell Patrick to fuck off.

Jen, plus husband and menu-wielding babe had just returned from holiday in Rome so I had opportunity to regain ground by telling my story about how as a sixteen-year-old schoolboy I'd borrowed money from a newsvendor near the Trevi Fountain.

Getting there at all had been a miracle. Mum and Dad certainly didn't have the money but the term before, I'd won the school essay prize, a substantial sum and more than enough to pay for the trip.

'We were on a school trip; thirty of us and two long-suffering teachers. We stayed at a hostel in the suburbs run by nuns who locked the doors at 10.00pm. Two of us went into town on the bus and spent part of the evening drinking wine and listening to the jukebox in a café. We'd been issued with only so much pocket money each day so we didn't blow the lot at once, and when we found we were a few lire short of the return bus ride we asked a newsvendor to help us out, insisting that we'd come back the next evening to pay him back. Much to our astonishment he gave us the lire, and much to his astonishment we returned the following evening and paid him back.'

There was silence.

'Full marks for honesty!' It was the first time Martinique had spoken to the whole group.

The girls looked at one another while breathing in unison through their noses. Then stared at me as if they hadn't believed a word. Their blank looks became smirks until the two of them turned into a laughing unit of condemnation.

There was no pudding. Instead, Martinique produced large brilliantly coloured ceramic bowls containing apples, pears, and a multitude of fruits of which I wasn't even sure of the names. There was a magnificent fresh pineapple which – as I had never had that either – I studiously avoided, instead selecting for myself a rather small dusty-looking apple.

'It's a russet!' Denise was leaning across the table and whispering to me.

'Oh.'

There was cheese, arranged over at least three wooden boards. I looked around for crackers but couldn't see any so cut myself a finger of what looked like Caerphilly but no doubt it was the produce of Languedoc cheesemakers. I didn't dare ask.

Coffee appeared served in a cafetière. It was strong and I was liberal with the milk. Denise had hers black and seemed to drink it down quite quickly.

'Mocha Sidamo,' mouthed Patrick staring at her as she did so, clearly enjoying the number of 'O's in the name.

'Could I have another of those please?' Denise held out her cup.

'It'll keep you awake,' I said clumsily and a little spoil-sportishly. She gave one of her throaty chuckles and looked at Patrick. His lips formed a daffodil trumpet shape.

Denise moved her head closer to whisper to Patrick, and

once again I had a view of the terrace and the erect carving knife with its blade buried in the teak tray. It was not yet dusk and the light was scintillating on its steel edge. I knew why, and I could feel the vibration in the floor beneath me. It was the underground trains… of course '…*when they were tunnelling for King's Cross…*' I looked up through the roof light at a passing airliner – they'd been up there doing that every ninety seconds since 0430hrs and wouldn't stop until 2330hrs and I'd been sitting down here oblivious. What was beneath the canal, and beyond the crevices in the brick walls of the house? There was a world wider than our little soiree with its talk of dropped stitches, the wrong way to eat asparagus, and whether or not I really had scrounged lire from a newsvendor, or whether Denise had really been to Glyndebourne. For the present anyway, I was happy to belong to both of those worlds.

THIRTEEN

I did not enjoy visiting the basement of the house. It wasn't just the smell coming from the inspection chamber, nor the knowledge that far beneath my feet were watery culverts and fume-filled chambers. It could be that what unsettled me was the low ceiling, the lack of daylight, the proximity to the neglected garden which imbued it with an air of oppression.

Or perhaps it was simply the way I was looking at things. The more I recalled my dream, and the more I scrutinized the accumulation of *déjà vu* events, the further I became convinced that I was being subjected to some kind of paranormal diversion. I'd known people at college who had held séances on wobbly card tables, had dabbled in automatic writing, and people who had boasted of things far darker and more dangerous than either. Of course, my thinking was daft, nothing of the sort was going on and I should pull myself together and get on with the job I was here to do; to run the office.

But it wasn't unreasonable that as a sensitive sort of intuitive guy who was hip to the way the house might have been used over its two-hundred-year life I was merely indulging my imagination on the kind of kitchen gossip that might have taken place down here. There were cupboards and drawers, fittings from the eighteenth century and empty of physical objects but most likely full of memories. There were nooks and crannies containing unspoken messages of past liaisons, alcoves where perhaps punishments had been carried out, and as I descended the stone stairs I jumped at the sight of a figure standing at the bottom in front of the photocopier.

'Hello, Al.'

My voice sounded surprised. It was Monday morning ten o'clock and he didn't look good.

'… Hello.'

'Are you all right?'

'I'm a bit hung-over.'

'Can't you go back to bed?'

'It's not that type of hangover.'

'What type *is* it then?'

'Nervous… got to get up… copy these fashion drawings.'

'But you're on holiday.'

'Not really, it was a deal with dad – when I swapped courses – that I do the degree in two years, that means working through most of the holiday.' His voice sounded as if it was in danger of disintegrating altogether.

'I see. I'm impressed at your perspicacity…' I said it in what I imagined was a pseudo toffee-nosed voice. '… I'm also impressed that you've got the hang of that zoom function, I haven't.'

'Easy, main menu, button 'A'; then scroll down.'

'You sure you're okay?' I'd witnessed hangovers like that

before… Perfectly balanced young men pacing the room, hearts hammering, insisting on being taken to A&E. I'd wondered whether he was going to have a panic attack but demonstrating the zoom function seemed to have calmed him a bit.

'The thing is… Dad, have you seen him this morning?'

'You're allowed *some* holiday, surely?'

'I'm not sure what kind of mood he's going to be in.'

I recalled the scene with the carving knife.

'It was my twenty-first last night.'

'Oh! Congratulations.'

'Well it didn't go quite to plan…'

Evidently Patrick had booked Langleys Bar whose staff had laid on a buffet – predominantly carnivorous – for him and Martinique, the twins, and a mere fifty of Al's friends who had each been issued with printed invites. As the evening progressed, more of Al's friends plus hangers-on kept arriving until the bar was packed with two hundred. As it was Sunday there was no proper security arrangement, and the few staff remaining were unable to cope. Many of the gatecrashers were helping themselves from the bar; others had arrived already swigging from bottles they'd been carrying in the street. The hall porter had attempted to stem the flow by locking the revolving doors, but a crush built outside. Someone claimed they needed to leave in an emergency so the door had to be opened again.

Patrick was delighted. He was about to give a speech, and an audience of two hundred plus would almost certainly do it justice.

'Jesus, it was embarrassing…' Al was looking over his shoulder and up the stairs in case there was the creak of leather brogues about to descend to the basement. '… It wasn't about me, it was all about him!'

The speech – it transpired – had contained phrases such as 'rite of passage', words such as 'sturdy', 'thrusting', and 'decisive' had occurred at frequent intervals. There had been a dire warning 'zero tolerance of failure', and an enigmatically chilling reference to 'bull's blood'. 'I personally will be still roaring at ninety,' Patrick had informed the mass of cheering, booing, and football rattling youth.

'It was like Dad was on steroids!' Al's voice had risen so high it must have been audible from the top of the stair. I put my finger to my lips in a rather bossy gesture.

'You know he flunked architecture school?' said Al as if desperately trying to change subject. I did vaguely. 'He went to work for Varcellus in California. That's all the public remembers so it didn't matter. That's why he's so intolerant of failure.'

What was worrying Al wasn't that the party had been gatecrashed, it was the fact that the two hundred insurgents had left the building before Patrick had finished his speech and with Al crowd-surfing on their upturned hands.

'I didn't want to go, they forced me. It was great though, we went to a warehouse party – there were several hundred there. It was fantastic music… it wasn't *just* the music it was the way the DJs were playing it. Warehouse music they call it – some people just say 'house music'. It's the thing in Chicago.'

I'd been to the Hacienda when it opened a couple of years ago – hardly anybody there. A lot of people didn't like it – '*Ooo ah dorn't lahk this… loouks lahk an aerporrrt carrr parrrk.*'

'It gets packed now,' insisted Al, 'the "Haci" was ahead of its time.'

'Is that *yooou,* Al?' A voice sounded down the stairs.

'Do you want me to hide you, is there a rear exit?' I whispered.

'No!' I replied loudly to the disembodied voice from upstairs.

Something furry brushed my trousers and swaggered up the stone stairs. A second later I heard Lauren's voice.

'Hellowe, Mackerel!'

When I got back upstairs I went into the butler's pantry office and found Lauren typing away. She was talking to Bea who was standing with her back to the window.

'Have you seen Al?' Lauren looked up at me.

'Not for a while.'

'Have you seen *Da-ad*?' Bea asked. Her expression was not dissimilar to the one Patrick had used when he made his – no doubt legendary by now – remark about asparagus.

'Briefly…'

'Did he mention Langleys? I've been telling Lauren…' Lauren looked at me with the kind of expression which might accompany an announcement of disinheritance, and containing the message that somehow, *I* was responsible.

Bea left the room and slammed the front door behind her without saying anything further. I was glad. I was also glad that I had met both Bea and Jen at the same time when five minutes later the front door opened and Jen came in. Had I not done so then I would have wondered why 'she' was asking me the same question twice.

'Have you seen *Da-ad*?' I felt like a fish in a small tank swimming around with no chance of escape.

'Briefly…'

'Did he mention Langleys?'

'No… Not on babe duty then?' I asked cheekily changing the subject.

'He's at nursery… almost three now. Then we've got Suzi, the au pair, so frees me up nicely to get on designing power stations. How's GI Group going?' I was probably imagining it but her emphasis on the words 'GI' sounded a little disparaging.

'Good… I'm going to need at least one assistant.'

'Oh, Dad won't like that. I've heard that they've got a woman CEO and good for her. That's why Dad didn't want anything to do with it… doesn't want a woman telling him what to do.'

'I see.'

'… Must dash.'

'Me too…' The front door slammed and Jen was gone.

'Fancy a drink later?' The voice was once again a conspiratorial whisper. I did.

Well '*Da-ad*' was going to have to lump it because any moment now there would be a knock on the front door and it was going to be Przemyslaw – Polish according to Lauren – who I would be interviewing and would hopefully be my man to help with GI Group.

The person who I opened the front door to looked as if he'd come straight from doing national service in the South African army; khaki cargoes, matching open-necked pilot shirt, desert boots, and blond hair styled in a feather cut and resting on top of both his ears.

'Hello.'

'Jim!', at least that's what I heard him say. What he'd *actually* said was 'Shem'.

'It's unpronounceable so people call me "Shem" – nearest English pronunciation is *Shemiswaaf.*'

'Okay, come in, come in!'

He'd answered my advert in BD but I'd done research on him and been told he was 'shit hot'. We sat in the main studio, me facing the window while he leafed through his work. He didn't smile and I got the feeling that he thought I wasn't the slightest bit interested in what he had to show me, which – given the strength of the reference I already had – was true.

What was making me edgy was what Patrick was going to say, how the two of them would get on, and my confidence on that score wasn't being helped by what I was picking up about him. He lived on the eighteenth floor of a council tower block in Finsbury Park, was an active member of the Socialist Worker Party, swore by 'eel pie-n-mash', and judging by the amount of sniffing, foot-tapping, and grimacing he was doing he either had some sort of drug habit or he didn't think much of what he saw, me included.

The thought occurred to me that given my background *I* could easily be *him*. I didn't think there was a cat in hell's chance of him taking the job if I offered it, and he wasn't going to be easy to handle, but I needed somebody quickly. Either I could search further, and lose time, or I could take a calculated risk and go along with the copper-bottomed reference. I offered him the job and, much to my surprise, he took it.

It was the Stag and Rifle again. I didn't mind. I preferred walking uphill to down. After no more than a week at Lloyd Lewis Associates I was beginning to get used to Lauren's notion of 'up here' and 'down there' – her 'down there' would mean W4 of course, but I did wonder how Belgravia fitted in with that classification.

Outside the house the air was better, and the higher you climbed the fresher it became. That didn't apply to the lower three stories of the house of course but even after this short time I'd found that I'd stopped noticing the foetid stench. I'd wondered whether it was just me. Denise hadn't mentioned it, but what about my other friends – parties at weekends? Had I begun to carry this smell around with me, like a goatherd might have a peculiar scent, or a fishmonger? Is it Caliban who perpetually smells of fish? Was it going to be occupational in the way that a plumber reeks of ozone, electricians are accompanied by an acrid burning, or archivists who give off the claustrophobia of hammered vellum?

It was warm, had been raining, and once again I could smell jasmine, mock orange, and honeysuckle, but this time I was aware of the sourness of mahonia blossom. It was growing in the border directly opposite the front door of the pub where last week the denim-clad red-headed male had been standing.

I studied the pub sign which I hadn't taken in during our previous visit. It was a skilful reinterpretation of David Hockney's 1975 *Kerby (After Hogarth) Useful Knowledge* which contains a series of perspective impossibilities. In the original Hockney – or Hogarth, whichever you like – an innkeeper's wife is shown leaning out of a first-floor window holding a taper and lighting the pipe of a shepherd who is standing on a hill a mile away. The Stag and Rifle's artist had shown the same woman pointing a rifle which appeared to be an inch away from the head of an out-of-scale stag standing on a snow-covered mountain top, five miles away. Separating the two subjects was a complex system of rivers, ravines, evergreen trees, and the mountains had the look of oyster shells stacked on the ice of a fishmonger's stall. Something familiar about the landscape gave me a small wave of nausea.

I'd taken the precaution of telling Lauren that I would be 'going on somewhere afterwards' so she didn't think I was hankering after another free taxi ride halfway home. She also seemed to have been thinking ahead and announced that she was going on to Highgate… A relief as it meant that when we left we would each be walking to different tube stations.

'… Two ESP!' Her fingers shot up in a victory sign to the barman as we edged our way through the mass of bodies. I was about to try and shoulder across to collect them while she found a seat when she added. '… It's okay he'll bring them, hmm.' We sat down – same banquette seats. The stags' heads were louring down at me, unsurprisingly with the identical expressions as on our previous visit.

How the place could be so packed at six o'clock on a Monday evening I couldn't fathom. They didn't seem to be the same people as last week either – less blue denim, more Samsonite, reps no doubt, and perhaps of the heat-seeking variety. The Loyal Order of Moose wasn't meeting because the notice read, *The Whixall Peat Moss Residents' Association Meeting will begin promptly at 6.00pm.*

There was a narrow gallery with a dark-oak balustrade running off the stairwell above which I'd failed to notice last week. One of the bar staff, an untrendy moustachioed youth wearing a white pilot shirt and shiny black trousers brought the two glasses of flat golden liquid and I paid.

'How's GI Group?'

'Well I think I've made a good start…'

'I bet you're dying to know about the twins.'

I was more interested to hear about Freia, but I had to admit that Bea and Jen had occupied more than the odd moment in my mind since the Asparagus Dinner.

'Bea looks *very* like His Lordship and Jen more like Freia – so you'd assume that Bea was more like Patrick in personality, yes?'

'That's what I'd thought,' I admitted.

'Well you'd be wrong. That's the mistake everybody makes. Jen's the quiet one, silent but deadly if you ask me… of course they're both loose cannons.'

If she were *really* asking me I'd say that they were both deadly, and both meticulously aimed cannons, but what I really wanted to ask her was how she knew what Freia's personality was like?

'Everybody's jealous of Freia – she's dead and she left a memory of a very warm loving person. Bea has this really weird idea that Jen is trying to recreate Freia by acting like her, yes.'

'Really…' Actually, I'd decided that the more free-spirited of the duo was Bea, the journalist, but I supposed that was the trap to which Lauren was referring. Twins I'd decided could be confusing in many ways. I wondered whether they were confusing to one another. Might they be suspicious of one another or could they be united in their suspicions of their father? I gave up... Imagine splitting twins? People had done it, not just governments, totalitarian regimes, but hapless warm-hearted adopting parents had done it to their cost and ended up being hated by both siblings.

'Bea looks sooo bullish. That's why she applied for architecture, hmm. As I'm sure you know, less than five per cent of architecture students are female so all the other students and people she ends up working with will see her as being quite masculine – you know, numerate, logical, scientific, convergent thinker – the usual crap assumptions, whereas in reality she's divergent-thinking, sensitive, creative, but more of a rebel. It was Jen who made the career decision first, so what did Bea come up with? Journalism, you can't get more rebellious than that.'

'I'll take your word for it.'

'Poor Al – it's short for Alain by the way, not Alan. Patrick and Freia always saw themselves as being cosmopolitan. You've probably realized that Al isn't Patrick's.'

I must have been gawping, I hadn't. 'Oh yes, Freia had an *extra-marital*. Everybody assumes, Patrick pretends, there's no proof that Al isn't legally his heir, but the fact remains that Al isn't of Patrick's blood. So, you can imagine how much he wants to impregnate Martinique. Al hasn't a clue, but one day the penny will drop when he realizes why he's so unlike Patrick, and when he finally succumbs to the disease of suspicion – catches it from the twins. You've seen the way they both look at him. "Where's it leading?" says Patrick to Al, "… you're living in a house with five girls, you need male company not a bloody fashion course!" The poor boy had had enough of architecture after a month, yes. For a start, he said that none of the people on the course had done an art foundation course – they'd all arrived straight from secondary school. Al had done a foundation course, Patrick wouldn't let the girls – said it was a waste of time but he made an exception "for the boy".

'Al told me their first project on the architecture course had been *Your Impressions of Tottenham.* Al had done this big expressive drawing in black wax crayon and the tutor had slated it saying it wasn't "cerebral". Then some smartarse straight out of grammar school turned up to the crit with this clear Perspex cube – which he'd got the technician to make – and inside was this sheep's head with its eyes pecked out… good job it was encased in Perspex because it would have been well stunk out. Evidently the student had said he'd just seen it lying there on a building site and he'd thought "essence of Tottenham", but Al said that he'd seen the same student coming out of a butcher's shop with a pink-stained paper parcel under his arm the day before the crit… Anyway, the tutor said it was the most "powerful and spontaneous piece of work the college had ever seen." Both the girls agreed with Patrick that Al should have seen the course through.'

'Did you do an art foundation course?'

'Lord, no… wanted to… Parents wouldn't allow. You're fortunate, hmm.'

Fortune wasn't the kind of thing I'd ever associated with me – particularly if you did a social comparison between me and Lauren. 'They're the gold standard Al says.'

'Gold?' I repeated stupidly.

'The art Foundation course is first real window onto the world – all secondary art education is shit.'

'So, what did *you* do?'

'English Lit degree… better than getting married and being presented to Her Maj.' She tapped her amber ring twice on the side of her beer glass – not the amber bit, the silver mounting. It made a high note which seemed to unite with a shrill female voice coming from the saloon. '… just joking,' she said. I knew she wasn't.

'… So here I am, literarily literate, but visually *il*literate.'

'I'd never thought of it that way.'

'I feel sorry for anybody who hasn't been to art college. That's ninety-nine per cent of the population who don't know what art is, and when you think about it not everybody who's been there knows what it is either – I mean what it's *for*.'

I had a horrible feeling she was going to ask me for a definition and I knew I hadn't got one. But then when you *did* art you didn't need to prove it.

'People I went to school with thought art was icing on a cake. Oh, we all loved Mrs Blake the art teacher, swore how we'd got into the souls of Constable, Caravaggio, or Brueghel after staring at their work in the National Gallery, but to really *feel* you have to *do*, you can't be told about art, you have to experience it for yourself. You can't fake creativity, hmm! And that state of visual illiteracy sometimes includes art critics.

'You know the kind of thing; Westminster School, reads English at Christchurch, becomes art critic for a respectable broadsheet newspaper, but never been near an art college… Invents a specialism – say Caravaggio's *Supper at Emmaus*. He wows the public with words, facts, but never feeling. He's no idea what it feels like to be a painter because he's never done it.'

A pearl of perspiration appeared from beneath her bobbed hair. It hovered for a second on her cheek bone, slid down cheek, chin and neck where it nestled in the small concavity next to her collar bone.

'You could take up painting, sculpture, printmaking, photography – go to evening classes?'

'What like a fucking Sunday painter? I demand total immersion!' I coughed hard to stifle a laugh at her born-again-Christian fervour.

'You never understand art until you actually *do* it, and once you've done it you'll find you don't *need* to understand it, because it's beyond intellect.'

She was telling me amazing things I hadn't realized. How did she know anyway? I was supposed to be the artist.

'At least if you did a course you'd be *doing* instead of ranting.' I thought she'd bite my head off but she smiled.

'I know I'm repressed in my thinking, but so are ninety-eight per cent of the population... I mean just how liberal was *your* upbringing?'

I thought of mum and dad, thought of them working ten-hour days, six days a week. Thought of how their only social outlet had been the local church which they felt they couldn't take part in because they were so exhausted after working to put food on the table. Karl Marx's calculation of the amount it costs to clothe, feed, and transport a person to their place of employment set against the value of their productivity, still in the 1960s, put my parents firmly into the category of the exploited.

But I'd never for one moment resented that or considered turning myself into a political animal. Sure, opportunity was something you had to battle for, but it *was* there, it *did* exist. It was back to the idea of the dream. I had the dream, mum had the dream; dad hadn't, it wasn't that it wasn't there to be dreamt, it was that dad simply thought dreams were something you forgot about the minute you woke up, that lakes were full of fish for catching, and water was for sailing on, or drinking. He didn't realize that lakes could be 'bottomless' or that if you looked through glass you could spy the heavens. It seemed also that neither did Lauren's parents.

'Did you know just how rude and stupid George V was about art? Not just him, all the rest of the bloody royals and their hangers on! People called Prince Charles a philistine a few weeks ago when he said that the proposed scheme for the National Gallery extension looked like "a carbuncle on the face of a well-known friend", but he's not. He makes an effort to understand, gets people interested, puts something back in, and he paints – even if he *is* a bit of a Sunday painter. Once you do art you'll never see reality in the same way again.'

'Take a sabbatical – I mean do the art foundation course, they take mature students. There's nothing stopping you.'

She looked at me wearily as if there *was* something stopping her, something that I couldn't and wouldn't comprehend.

'Do you ever consider that you won't be rubbing shoulders with arty types for ever?' She was scrutinizing me as if she had just parted the bushes and found me cowering there like some rarified creature. 'Think of those ninety-nine per cent. One morning you'll wake up and find yourself surrounded by people who think that art is a waste of time and money and should be abandoned in favour of charitable work, like the Elizabethans who believed that a mind that wasn't "being educated" was doing no more than playing, and its body should be beaten until it did something "worthwhile". Rednecks who say, "my three-year-old daughter could do that" – perfectly intelligent and well-educated people who should know better, but because they haven't *done* art they don't. You'll be a lone voice and you'll think of that piece of smartarse student graffiti, *Earth without art is "eh", you know E-H!* Even Neanderthal Man had art, yes!'

She repeated the 'eh' sound this time giving it a sub-human sound like the gurgling the murky water might have made as it passed far below our feet when we stood in the Butler's Pantry. She sat back and took a long swig of ESP. The light coming down the stairwell gave her neat bobbed hair the oddest green tinge – the colour of Welsh slate.

A door slamming on the gallery made me look up and a man with a big nose and curly black hair came cantering down the stairs looking as if he was about to burst into tears.

'Patrick sent all the kids to comprehensives, yes.'

'Did he? … Surprises me.'

'Why?'

'He could afford to choose private.'

'Exactly… He chose comprehensive. He *wants* people to make choices, likes to think he's handing people opportunity. It's the way he does it that can hurt, hmm.'

I noticed that she was suddenly looking quite small. Her limbs seemed to have folded up as if she'd tidied them away for the day. Parts of her looked young, others seemed to speak of an eternity and I became aware for the first time that her eyes had the look of a very old person… Difficult to imagine those eyes sitting in the head of the Baby Lauren and easy to visualize them unchanged when on her deathbed – if she ever died that was.

'It's the snobbery,' I ventured. No doubt she'd had an account of the put-downs at the Asparagus Supper.

'He's got a thing about British institutions – of which I've a morsel or two of knowledge meself, hmm,' she added with a kind of calculated modesty. 'You'll have had the "do you go to Sadler's Wells and Covent Garden, or are you one of these Met people?" There isn't any establishment he hasn't researched; the Proms, Wimbledon, Goodwood, Brands Hatch, the Chelsea Flower Show. He's recently graduated to "Glasto", even though it was only to pick up the twins, but to give him credit he did get into the spirit of it by dressing in black.

'He can also play the people's man by talking long and loud about Arsenal, darts, and the origins of the *Sun* newspaper, yes. If you openly accuse him of snobbery he'll turn on you and meticulously prove that it's really you who is the snob. That's the essence of Patrick. He sculpts himself larger than life because he knows that Andy Warhol is right, *real* human emotions look small and insignificant compared with the emotions in films or literature. So, if you're prepared to tolerate the bogus you can begin to understand where he's coming from, yes?'

The door on the gallery above burst open and a male figure hurtled through it; steadied itself against the oak balustrade. The door was slammed by an unseen hand and the man gingerly made his way downstairs towards us. Like the previous man he had a big nose and black curly hair and I noticed that there was a trickle of blood between his nose and mouth. As he reached the foot of the stairs he paused as if he was going to speak to us… Seemed to change his mind and walked through the bar and out into the sunshine where I could see him standing in front of the mahonia bush.

'… Then there's the rumpen-lumpen part of the population which is little better than the Nazis when it insists that art should be beauty, yes.'

She'd changed tack again. She was a master at laying down one idea on top of another – walking away, then coming back, picking one idea up, putting another one down. '… A view which comes from the State, be it Roman, Greek, Egyptian – or early twentieth-century Australian; it's simply just one idealised perception of human or equine beauty and it ignores the value of experimentation, failure, serendipity, and insists that only the end result matters, never the process, hmm.'

I was amazed how much thought she'd put into the subject. I couldn't begin to summon up arguments like these, but then again, I was a do-er of art, not a thinker about it.

'… How did your interview with your new man go?'

'Oh, I think he's right…'

'… Polish.'

'He's born here… seems quite left wing, Jack-the-Lad almost, I'm really not sure how he's going to get on with Patrick…'

'Behind every Pole is a pretty interesting story, hmm.'

'Really?' I'd met only two Poles, one at college, another at my first job. They'd both had extravagant moustaches, and each struck me as being rather conceited. I'd heard of martial law, had a vague idea of who Jaruzelski was, and that was it… Lauren it seemed was a mine of information.

'… For a start, there are two Polands, one, the Polish People's Republic, a Stalinist puppet set up in 1945, and two, the international culture of the years between 1918 and 1939 with all its complex pockets of feudalism, class divides… with Warsaw an artistic, philosophical, and scientific nucleus to rival Paris, Berlin, Vienna and whose government plus a core of upper-middle-class Poles which packed its bags – including all its gold – and came to London when the Nazis invaded…'

'Gold?' I repeated stupidly.

'Gold. They smuggled it out on a train in 1940 across the parts of Europe which were already occupied, and right under the noses of the Nazis, to London where they set up the Government in Exile, yes.'

I was amazed… Gold, governments in exile? It was news to me.

'…When the war ended these émigrés couldn't return and those who did "disappeared" because they'd "had contact" with the West. This guy may be well be streetwise, switched on – and so forth, but it's unlikely he's the working-class London lad he makes out he is… Chances are he's the son of one of these aristocratic refuges hiding in plain sight.'

'What happened to the gold?'

'Well it certainly didn't go back east so… must be still here somewhere…'

'… Really?' I still didn't have much of a clue what she was talking about but it was certain that there was more to the guy than I'd thought. The chemical mix between the four of us was going to interesting.

'He's quite sullen.'

'He hasn't got Patrick's charm then? Oh, I know Patrick's

got charm, but what *is* charm?' She'd switched again, and I felt she was laughing at me.

'... If it's flattery then it's nothing but a weapon to arm the flatterer and can be fatal for the flattered. If it's a form of enchantment then it's a method of removing the power of freewill from the enchanted and therefore *also* ultimately fatal. If it's being "nice" to people in the sense of being "agreeable" then Patrick just doesn't do either nice or agreeable.

'But he won't shout you down, he'll listen to your argument, then he'll add the finishing touch, *his* touch. He's a good orchestrator, he likes to get ideas from other people then get them to pluck the fine strings, it's funny really, his form is logic but his essence is confusion... Same again?'

She leaned forward, placed her empty glass on the table tapping the side of it with her amber ring. I rose ready to go to the bar but the young man with the moustache appeared, took our glasses, disappeared, and returned with them refilled all in the space of what seemed no more than seconds. This time she paid.

'You've noticed his mouth?'

'The "O"?'

'... More than that. It's almost an autonomous organism. It indulges in all sorts of little movements; truncated earthworm, a mollusc engaged in its mating ritual, the engorged penis of some mammal, or a sea animal reacting when threatened. His oral flexings aren't just visual, there are noises you may have noticed; tiny squeakings, creakings, fizzings, chirrupings. But these *kissy kissy* sounds aren't an expression of tenderness, they're a prelude to a fucking bollocking!'

Her voice had risen and several heads had turned in our direction. 'It's Patrick's unique style of *bienseance.*' Once again, she sat back, calmer now.

'Who is Uncle Falco?'

'Ah, now you're asking!'

At least this time she sounded as if she wasn't going to tear me off a strip.

'… Client, restaurant-owner who claims to create Milanese food but has the temperament – if not the birth – of a Sicilian… Which reminds me, Patrick – you will have noticed – has adopted an *estilo culto* through words and pronunciations, which might seem perfectly at home in the mouth of a native, but coming out of his, sound artificial… I mean, does he really need to say *Milano* all the time? We're in London for fuck's sake. He's always on about "the British weather" but the way he behaves reminds me of the British holidaymaker returning from Bali who is determined to show the rest of the British public how he went *native* and – in spite of metallic skies and freezing temperatures – determinedly pads off the Gatwick Express still wearing his sarong and flip-flops, yes.'

I hadn't been to Bali, but I had frequently noticed folk standing in the rain outside Victoria station wearing sombreros.

'If Patrick were being interviewed by Joan Bakewell…' she rambled on '– or whoever – and was asked the question "what are your two greatest loves in life?" he would reply "beautiful women and good food". His confidence in giving such an answer would stem from the fact that he wouldn't be speaking for himself – oh no, to do that would be arrogant and egotistical. By giving such an answer, he would be no more than acting as spokesman for the entire human race... Women and food are – after all – no more than the basic requirement for Man's survival, and procreation. He would be demonstrating his loyalty to humanity, yes.

'You know, Pulse...' She looked straight at me with her thousand-year-old eyes.

It was the first time I'd heard her use my name. '... You could make a real difference here – I mean really change things... Look I *must* go!'

'Oh, I won't be in tomorrow. I'm going to meet my mother at Victoria coach station.'

I thought I detected a smile.

What I'd said was true but it was 5.00pm before I was due at Victoria. I would be taking an early train from Euston and heading north to get the rest of that telephone number.

FOURTEEN

Y ou look familiar.

I'm on the train, thinking about the twins. What a handful! Never split them – if you're planning to adopt that is…The man – or woman who comes between kin is in for a rough ride, as PL Travers – the inventor of Mary Poppins – found to her cost.

Travers, forty, husbandless and childless decides to adopt. Why not? She can afford to bring up a kid on her own. It's twin boys from Ireland, but she only takes one and never tells him about the other one? Seventeen years later the Irish twin – who *has* been told he's got a sibling – turns up at her Chelsea house demanding to see his brother. She sends him packing. Then the first twin comes back, gets wind something's going on, goes and looks in every pub on the King's Road, and finds twin number two. They go back to the house, play merry hell and clear off together with number one twin ending up disowning Travers.

I'm imagining what it would be like looking for a twin. If it's a case of a choice of six pubs on the King's Road then the task wouldn't be too formidable. It's just looking for someone who looks similar, couldn't be simpler. Any of us could have one – I mean a twin we hadn't been told about, which is why I'm so fascinated by the head opposite me.

The head in front of me is resting, tilted back on the train seat headrest. I know it's not asleep because the eyes are open. The hands appear to be at prayer, but only for a split second as they come together. Between the palms is a broadsheet newspaper and as the page is turned the hands part, the face disappears and once again I can see the name of the paper – the *Telegraph*.

I'm playing at being a spy, because when I look in the train window I can see the man's reflection, clearly. The head which seems to hover above the passing fields is more distinct than the head which is momentarily revealed to me every four minutes when the pages are turned, and it's this head which appears to me to be not unlike my own.

Ah! The palms come together and this time with an air of finality. I see the vertical sliver of paper collapse on itself. The man squeezes his fingers along its folded edge, knocks it into a flat rectangle, dusts it with the back of his hand – as if removing crumbs from its surface – and places it on the table in front of him. You do look familiar, and about my age. The Justice with fair round belly – except it's not *that* round.

The funny thing is your face is still indistinct. You look like a man who's not quite his own master, which is perhaps why the image of the head outside the carriage window seems so much clearer than the one inside.

The couple sitting next to us are French. Oh God! I can almost hear you say it. It's not that the man's arrogant or that the woman seems to be too submissive, it's that like me you just don't know what the fuck they're talking about. Not speaking a second language always makes me feel like a provincial. Everyone in London seems to be capable of bursting into a foreign tongue without the slightest provocation, but not me, oh no! What makes it worse is that she's clearly a fluent English speaker because when she's not talking to her Frenchie partner she's reading *Cosmopolitan*. I think that like me you are a northerner and quite possibly you're on your way home.

I smile. Not an invitation sort of smile, not a personal kind, one of those ambiguous sort of smiles, which *could* be directed at the person sitting opposite you, but a smile more likely to be purely for one's own consumption. You sigh and look straight at me.

'It's now or never…' you say. I agree. 'The crunch has come,' you say. You couldn't be putting it better, I think. 'There's a limit to how far a man can be pushed.' Your priorities are spot on, there's no denying it.

'I'm going to have it out with my boss.'

Your spectre outside the carriage window merges with red brick as the train slows into Nuneaton station. The aisles of the carriage are packed with people standing. We're in the last set of seats at the end of the carriage, and I can just see the WC door wedged open, a man wearing an MUFC shirt sitting on the toilet pan drinking cans of beer, the lobby piled high with huge nylon holdalls. Nobody leaves the train.

'Is it just *this* boss you don't get on with?' I ask impertinently.

'They've all been bloody difficult,' you snap. You're right.

'It's all about the basic pupil–master relationship.' I sit

up in my seat, paying you every attention now. 'The master is always jealous of his pupil,' you're so adamant.

'Not proud then – I mean if they do well?'

'They might say they're proud, but there's this basic fear.' You may have got something there. I must be frowning and I can see you're thinking that I need more explanation, and I have a distinct feeling you're going to give it me.

'Titian feared that Peterzano would become more successful than him, and we know for definite that Peterzano was green at the gills about Caravaggio's achievements. Pieter Brueghel 1 was always worried that Pieter Brueghel 2 would do better than him, Pieter Brueghel 2 was jealous of Pieter Brueghel 3, and Jan Brueghel was always in two minds about whether Ambrosius would do better than any of them. In the end, they could have all saved getting themselves into an untidy tizzy because PB 1 hung onto his reign as the family painting king. Then there's Joseph Albers and Robert Rauschenberg... and the Formbys...' Obviously an afterthought.

'What, George?'

'...They were both called George.'

'...The famous one?'

'Ah! *That* depends what you call fame.'

'...The one who played the banjo.'

'Ukulele actually...'

'All right, ukulele.'

'Ah! But they both played ukuleles.' You look smug. 'The point I'm making is that the *leaning on the lamp post* one we've all heard of stole his father's clothes.'

'...Really?'

'...Well, stole his father's act – the hat, the ukulele, the grin, the double entendres. The reason we know George the younger is TV and radio. His father was the bigger star, got paid more, and got a much grander monument to him in Warrington churchyard. Wee George just gets a tiny inscription. Dad died young, before George the younger launched his career. You can imagine the professional rivalry if he hadn't popped it when he did. Not getting on with your boss is career envy, believe you me.'

'Ere, you two!' I look up and see the red-faced man in the MUFC shirt looking down at me, hands supporting himself on the table top '… Yer, *you* two…' He stares beerily, from me to you. He's vacated his porcelain throne and he's squeezing his way down the aisle giving audience to whoever's eye he catches. Again… 'You two, you're like two peas in a pod, two eggs in a box.' He wrenches his red hands away from the table and continues his swaying journey.

You go back to your newspaper. When we arrive at the station you're standing right behind me as we shuffle along waiting to leave the train. Once I've climbed down onto the platform I look round to say goodbye but you've vanished.

FIFTEEN

As I walked down the platform towards the barrier, two questions were nagging me. The first – what the hell was I doing here, in this northern city and quite likely heading for danger – was the easy one. Though I was here by the sheer force of compulsion, the logical side of my brain was aware that almost certainly I was *not* going to prove or solve a crime. I wasn't a detective and had no intention of playing at being one.

I wasn't going to be doing any record-checking on Freia's death, or funeral, I wouldn't have known where to start. I was following a lead which by sheer chance had been revealed to me, that was all. I had two choices; i) ignore it and spend the rest of my life speculating as to what might be the connection between Freia and Hood, ii) give in to my curiosity and get nearer to the truth. I had chosen number two.

The second imponderable was the existence of Lloyd Lewis Associates. One person I'd talked to had described it as 'a practice run *for* gentlemen *by* gentlemen,' and I could see why. Patrick's previous crew had obviously abandoned ship and it wasn't difficult to see why that had happened. But why carry on when it wasn't a source of income to him? Wouldn't he be better clearing off to one of his tax havens, or retiring to look after his vineyards… And what about Lauren? She couldn't type; she was supposed to be a writer but didn't seem to have published anything, and the treatment from Patrick! Why did she put up with it? She had *means*.

In spite of her abruptness – which I took to be a characteristic of the upper classes – and general strangeness, there was something about her I liked, but I couldn't decide whether the tittle-tattle in the pub was revenge on Patrick, or whether I was being fed information for a specific reason. I'd begun to wonder if the practice existed solely for Patrick's pleasure. A menagerie of strange animals, and his own private theatre where comedy and tragedy were to be acted out by unsuspecting individuals. I had begun to fear that perhaps Patrick was a magnet and I a hapless iron filing.

As I stepped down onto the station platform I was praying that I would be back on this very spot in not much more than half an hour. It would take me ten minutes to get to Brazzers in a taxi and my heart was going like a bongo. I could barely hear the loudspeaker announcements which flooded into one another as I hurried across the concourse to the taxi rank. A few feet in front of me a tall black guy with a 'fro' dropped a king-size bottle of Coke onto the tarmac, its plastic cracking and its contents foaming angrily across the pavement.

Sitting in the back of the cab on the acrylic plaid rug inhaling the air freshener, the enormity of what I was doing struck me. I had no business to be going to Brazzers, and if I was caught, no explanation no matter how ingenious would save me. There was no Plan B; I would have to take the consequences.

Just because there was no Plan B, didn't mean to say that I didn't have a Plan A. I'd brought along my own wad of fake mail – junk I'd been collecting for a week. As I entered the Formica-lined office I would wave it at the girl on the desk as I sailed through, and on to Hoodie's office. I'd reckoned that I could be in and out of the building in under four minutes. No doubt an insurance underwriter would have a formula by which they could calculate my level of risk, but for me it was going to be all about confidence, that and a quiet prayer that Hood – or Dickson – were not on the premises.

I could see the taxi driver scrutinising me in his mirror. To give my journey plausibility I'd told him that I was an interior designer – doing some work at the club.

'Ahh, interior design, I know!'

He said it as if he'd just identified a particular football team or a make of car. '…Wood floor, white walls, downlighters; that's it, isn't it?' A smile of recognition appeared on his face like a quiz contestant who, confident that he'd given the right answer, knew that the prize would soon be his.

'I suppose so,' I conceded.

He seemed to be driving like hell, down street after street of desperate pink terraces, past high walls that looked like prisons, through a wasteland of demolished buildings, past factories with castle-like towers, past cranes, past smoking fires. I could see the moors in the distance and I felt a sudden need to go to the lavatory.

Abruptly he veered left and I heard/felt the tearing of coke cinders under car tyres – heard the ratchetting of the handbrake.

'Can you wait please; I'll be fifteen minutes at most.'

'Pay me for what you've had and I'll wait.'

I paid, opened the door, stepped out, slammed, and crunched my way across the cinders. I glanced back at him, staring after me perhaps wondering why I hadn't gone in through the main door on the road. My heart was hammering.

I walked down the flight of calcined stone steps, double speed. Along the subterranean corridor of saliva-coloured glazed brick. There'd be no going to the toilet this time. I opened the steel-panelled door. Inside it was the same girl sitting at the desk, bottle-red quiff – shiny green fat-shouldered jacket. She was on the telephone.

'Mail for Mr Hood!' I waved the fan of bogus letters. 'I'll put them on his desk.' She didn't even look up. As I pulled open the door leading to the dimly lit corridor I was hit by a wave of adrenalin. Supposing Hood had seen me arrive and was following me, dragging his bad leg behind his good one?

I stopped at the painted door on my right, as if to sniff the air around me, and felt it with my hand just as I'd watched Dickson do, as if checking that it was sound. I *had* to knock, if Hood *was* in there I was fucked, but I had to know. Think positive! Think of that insurance risk assessment, the chances of him being in there were… I knocked… waited… silence. There was a squeak as I squeezed the aluminium handle, opened, and poked a light switch on the left-hand wall.

I closed the door behind me and crossed to the notice board. There was so much blood pounding through my head I could barely see the odds and sods of paper. There it was,

FREIA LLOYD-LEWIS 01– I fumbled for my notebook and copied it, my hand was shaking so much I wasn't even forming the numerals properly; 01-241-0167. I rammed the notebook back into my bag, strode towards the door, hand on the handle. I was listening – just in case – and I was sure I could hear the distant mewing of a cat. Gingerly I opened the door, closed behind me, and almost stopped dead. To my right where the corridor turned I could see on the wall an enormous shadow of a cat, tail erect and quivering. I heard a voice.

'Ellowe Stripy!'

I ran, ran on tiptoe, ran like Sir Giles in *The Hound of the Baskervilles* on the edge of the moor, and running for his life, I ran tugging open the door for the safety of the Formica office.

'Job done!' I yelled. The green and red figure was still on the phone.

I wrenched open the steel-clad outer door, and once past the window I broke into a sprint, past saliva-coloured bricks, up calcined stone steps, and back onto the cinders where I stopped in disbelief. The taxi had gone.

Again, I ran, across cinders, past stained and rusted containers and out onto the main road. I looked left but there was nothing, just moor. I looked right, along a seemingly endless wall of crumbling brick. I was on the edge of panic.

On the opposite side of the road I could see a bus shelter of steel and smashed glass. I ran over to it, dodged inside and crouched below the level of its window. I was now directly opposite the main entrance door to the club, double-panelled doors in dark wood, the name *Brazzers* a semicircle of pink neon above it. I prayed that I was invisible. There was no traffic, no people.

The chances of a bus seemed remote, and as I looked at my watch I was amazed to see it was still only just gone eleven in the morning. The taxi driver had just been nervous. Taking me to a club whose owner had a notorious reputation was one thing, waiting outside there for me to emerge was perhaps tempting providence too far.

There was a timetable, but illegible through glass which, like that of the shelter, was not only broken but seemed to have been smeared with a variety of substances that had the look of human bodily fluids. As I squatted trying to peer through the mess of the window and listening for a noise that might be a bus I saw a sight, heard a sound which caught my breath.

Emerging through the gap in the wall, like an oil slick crawling up a Saudi-Arabian beach, was a black Mercedes limousine. I could hear the cinders crunching under its tyres. If it turned left its occupant would not see me, if it came right and past the shelter I would be visible.

It sat there – no other traffic, so no flashing indicator. I looked at my watch; fifteen seconds, thirty, forty-five. One minute, one minute fifteen. It was Hood, it *had* to be, and somehow, he knew I was there, I could feel it... he was making me sweat. One minute thirty, one minute forty-five, two minutes precisely and the car lurched left and tore away towards the moor. I saw an orange and cream double-decker bus and I all but rushed out into the road in an effort to ensure it stopped.

I paid, sat down among the six old age pensioners on the lower deck and began to breathe normally. I had the number at last.

SIXTEEN

When I arrived back at Euston it was 2.30pm so I took the tube to Green Park and wandered about, looking for somewhere for late lunch. I'd been too full of nervous energy to eat anything up until now, but the feel of space in the park, the movement of the air, and the distant drone of traffic was beginning to calm me.

I found the café I'd remembered from some months before. It was timber with pointy roofs, criss-cross metal bracing and had a clunky wooden floor which gave it an odd atmosphere of impermanence. I decided I would sit outside at the timber-slatted tables in one of those aluminium-framed chairs with webbing made from thick red plastic.

Inside, the array of baguettes was formidable; avocado and bacon, stilton and beetroot, brie and walnut... I chose one containing giant shavings of very yellow cheddar smeared with pickle whose simple geometry of cubes and spheres spoke to me of Branston. Comfort rather than adventure was on the agenda after the stress of the morning.

I sat for what seemed ages, letting myself be part of the gentle hiss of the urban sanctuary of parkland. After munching and swallowing had ceased, and once again I had become aware of my breathing and of gravity, I felt ready to make my way to Victoria Station to meet Mum. I had shared the entire café during that time with only four other people. It was the height of season and I wondered what would happen to the leftover pickles, walnuts, bacon, beef, brie, and beetroot at the end of the day.

When I reached the edge of the park I started straight down Grosvenor Place, but as I was early I decided to backtrack and walked down Chester Street, along Wilton Mews, Wilton Street, to Upper Belgrave Street where I found myself lingering, looking across Eaton Square and wondering... It struck me that the colonnaded buildings in the square were bigger grander versions of what Lloyd Lewis's terrace had meant to be before its developer had run out of money – or succumbed to cholera. Except that the Eaton Square ones had been smeared with white stucco, like icing on an architectural cake designed to hide the imperfections beneath. The Georgians had been inveterate building bodgers. Of course, Lauren might not live there. She might have a garret, or even a basement which perhaps smelt of the Embankment.

I was glad I'd got to Victoria Coach Station early because Mum's coach was already sweeping in across the petrol-infused tarmac of the station floor. After Green Park, the air was unbreathable, and the reverberation of concrete and glass almost unbearable. The door of the coach opened and I could see Mum standing in the aisle shuffling slowly along; she hadn't seen me. She looked so small, and when she eventually appeared on the steps I noticed she'd bought herself a new dress. A dusty pink it made her look older than her sixty-seven years.

With her feet once again on tarmac she was full of the journey, knew *all* about the younger woman she'd been sitting next to, and appeared to have made friends for life.

'I like your new coat.' She'd bought a lightweight coat which she immediately donned as if to demonstrate its capabilities. It was azure – its finish even looked like the texture of the powder crushed from natural stone, and unlike the dress, it suited her.

'... Debenhams!' she whispered, as if it were a cut above... '... Soft touch – feel!'

I took her luggage from the bus driver.

'We'll get a cab.'

Mum would never call them by that name. She always said 'taxi' with the emphasis on the first three letters as if it represented a tithe she was being forced to pay to some powerful landowner. As she said it her breathing became short – partly the onset of heart disease, but also fear of the cost.

Once inside the cab she sat bolt upright, her eye never leaving the price meter, as if she were subjecting the meter needle to her will in order to prevent it from rising. She'd done the trip once before so knew where she was going – sort of.

Dad had died five years ago, so she'd been through the merry widow stage and had now begun to feel vulnerable – as to what the rest of it all, life, was going to be like. Unsurprisingly, travelling was the problem for her, and no wonder when it consisted of a five-minute taxi drive from her house to the coach pick-up, a four-and-a-half-hour coach ride, followed by an hour's taxi ride to my flat.

The cab chugged its way along Chelsea Embankment, north to Earl's Court, and west down Cromwell Road heading for Hammersmith, and beyond that W4. During the journey Mum hadn't a clue where we were, but she had an eye, and she also had a sixth sense of place.

'Isn't that where we got stuck in traffic last time? … Was that where we got held up by that Gay Pride march?' Sometimes she'd get it wrong… 'Aren't we near Flanagans?'

'No Mum, that was Baker Street,' …but more often than not she would get it right.

She held a firm belief that life in the Provinces was far more fast-moving and livelier than in London where – for the duration of her stay – seventy per cent of her time seemed to be spent sitting in the back of a taxi while she worried about the fare.

My experience chimed with that of my mother, but in a different way and for a different reason. If there were people in London who held liberated views on life then there were far more who were the most myopic people I'd ever met. London – I'd decided – possessed the most cliquey, most set-in-their-ways, and the most socially and professionally parochial minds possible.

'Fancy a nice electrical contract in NW3?' I'd offered a Battersea born and based contractor.

'Nah mate, fouzand pahnds just for driving over the river we want!'

But attitudes were changing. There was a multicultural society emerging, which was industrious. People from the Asian subcontinents, the Middle East, and very often it was the Poles – not the sons and daughters of the wartime émigrés, it was folk from the Polish People's Republic who Lauren had drawn my attention to. People who were coming over to better themselves, would work at anything, would travel anywhere. Were open all hours, open to new thinking... and of course open to exploitation, but that was another story.

When we arrived at the flat I made a cuppa to be going on with, and cooked chicken livers with onions. This was the kind of food my mother felt at home with, and it was the kind of food I felt at home preparing. She insisted on peeling potatoes, chopping the carrots and slicing the green beans. Afterwards she didn't want to watch television. 'Why, when I have this beautiful view to look at?'

I'd bought the flat two years previously, my first purchase. Two bedrooms, it was long and thin – like a one-sided railway carriage – and south-facing. There were parquet floors, a tiny 'U'-shaped kitchen, and a bathroom with white chunky-angled fittings and yellow and black tiles. I loved it.

It was on the third floor of a large four-storey – what estate agents called a 'mansion block'. Invariably I would leave my kitchen window open – probably not the most secure routine but, as there was a vertical gas pipe, it had saved me when I'd been locked out on at least one occasion. There were six hundred flats arranged in a triangle around a green space containing cherry trees. I'd discovered that they'd been built in 1938 and had been constructed with underground air raid shelters. You could see the concrete entrances in the sides of the earth redoubts, and I supposed that they'd blocked them up after the war.

It was a forgotten world which no longer seemed to belong in the 1980s. For a start, its location was odd, isolated from surrounding roads by two railway lines and the Great West Road which seemed to imprison it in a kind of W4

Bermuda triangle. The nearest shops were ten minutes' walk, which didn't matter to Mum so long as she knew where, and as long as there was a café where she could find people to talk to, she would be happy for the few days she would be staying.

Mum stared at the sun setting over the cherry trees, unpacked some of her things, stared at the cherry trees now ghosted against the dusk, unpacked the rest of her things, stared out into shadow upon shadow, and finally retired to bed. I'd told her that she might hear my voice on the telephone. 'Oh, that'll be nice,' she replied, perhaps assuming that at last I had acquired a girlfriend. She didn't know about Denise, and I wasn't prepared to tell.

Though Mum was in awe of London, she would sleep soundly in the knowledge that she was with her only son who was making his way in the world, and who had done far better than taking the job at Swifts. Living with her in the one-ended terrace until he got married and living in the Barrett house that she had always hoped he would inhabit. She'd been right about art college, and Dad had been wrong.

I took my notebook out of my attaché case, stared at the telephone number. It didn't ring the faintest of bells, but I could see by the prefix it wasn't the same location as the Lloyd Lewis house. I picked up the ivory-coloured plastic receiver, dialled and heard it ring out. I tensed. After five rings I felt myself relax, nobody was going to answer. On the sixth ring, there was a click.

'Hullow?' The voice was male, its speech rounded, its resonance breathless.

I'd been so keen to try the damn thing I'd forgotten to anticipate what might happen next. I hadn't planned anything.

'Patrick?'

I waited a second too long before reacting and whoever it was put the phone down. What a fool! I quickly worked out a patter, rehearsed, and dialled again… Again, the click, but this time all I heard was what might have been the drag on a cigarette, and its long exhaling… or was it merely the faint fizz of the space which is the telephone line between caller and recipient?

SEVENTEEN

It was 11.30am and I was sitting on the tube gazing through the open doors of the stationary train – at a poster advertising a forthcoming film *The Company of Wolves* – as the train paused at Knightsbridge. I'd changed from the District Line at Hammersmith and my plan was to get off at Green Park, walk down St James's Street, and along Pall Mall where I was to meet Patrick at 12.15, at his club.

The day was going to be an interesting one; lunch with Patrick, he then had a further meeting at his club while I would return to the office and work on GI Group until 6.00pm when Mum would arrive at Lloyd Lewis Associates. The intention was that I would show her round, we would have a modest bite to eat at the local Pizza Express and then return – via taxi – to W4.

'Pulse!' Patrick had raised his finger as if he were about to tell me the facts of life. '… Now you *will* be bringing your gal-*lant* mama to see me upstairs for a glass of wine.'

It was an order, and I knew that Mum wouldn't be missing it for the world. I tried to insist that she take a taxi from W4 to the Lloyd Lewis house but she was adamant that she would go on the bus. The mere notion of spending an hour occupying the same space as someone else, and being prevented from a continual flow of chatter by a glazed screen was not acceptable to Mum... And of course, there was the cost. With her pensioner's bus pass the entire journey would be free. The fact that it would mean three different buses and take at least two hours was immaterial. There would be friendships to be forged on the lower deck; it would be like a round-London sightseeing tour without all the twaddle.

As I sat on the tube I reran in my mind last night's telephone fiasco. I'd tried directory enquiries and of course they'd refused to give me the address without a name. They had however told me it was a Dalston prefix. I had a mental picture of the assortment of dingy properties over shops on the Kingsland Road and imagined a hardened killer in one of them, screwing and unscrewing the telescopic sights on his rifle... Or perhaps an oily brake-tampering mechanic lurking – even a smooth ex-public-school Armani-wearing assassin, listening to Beethoven on his state-of-the-art Duo Omega G2 loudspeakers. There *were* smart-ish properties in Dalston, here and there.

I knew where Patrick's club was because I'd walked past it many a time long before I'd even known him. I'd never been in because I'd never known anyone who was even remotely likely to possess such a membership. Patrick had given me instructions of how to get there, what to do, and in such purposeful and painstaking detail as to resemble a father explaining to his four-year-old the difference between nursery school and junior school.

I'd also never been in there because, although I admired the symmetry and proportion of that kind of architecture, to me it exuded exclusivity, formed a barrier of remoteness, and signalled a social divide. It was like the difference between the architecture of the 'closed' Scala Theatre Milan, and that of the 'open' Royal Festival Hall of London.

I was wearing a dark suit, dark tie, and as I mounted the steps leading up to the oak-panelled front door I felt reasonably confident that I would fit in. The porter, a man dressed just like me, seemed curious that I didn't have a mackintosh even though the sky outside was cloudless. I was asked to sign in by a registrar, also dark-suited, and scrutinizing me as if I were in the act of using a false name. There was a category – *'to see…'* The seated registrar could read upside down.

'Mr Lloyd Lewis will be with you shortly.' His voice had the timbre of utmost misery.

I tried not to, but I realized I was pacing up and down on the black and white chequered marble floor, as if I was a pawn being alternately placed and withdrawn by a hesitant chess player. I had to admit to myself that not only was I nervous, I was bursting with preconceptions and prejudice. The two men who had just 'processed' me were – to my mind – examples of humanity repressed by the Establishment, and forbidden to show even an atomic nudge of self-expression… Though ha, ha! I wasn't about to let myself fall into that cliché of a class argument, I was about to smash a myth and to smash a myth you first needed to follow one – i.e. that Establishment meant stuffy, repressive, and exclusive, while Alternative meant liberated, expressive, and inclusive.

The reception staff of Indie and avant-garde clubs and record companies I'd met and worked alongside had exhibited just as many signs of repression, were just as full of prejudice, pointless rules, and snobbishness. There was no real difference between the girls at Brazzers, the staff of Rap 52, or Dickson's Railway Arch club, and these men. All had their petty resentments and looked at the people they served as if they hated their guts. '… Duty and loyalty' to their employers? I don't think so. They behaved as if they were medieval serfs who had convinced themselves that they were irreconcilably tied to the land. 'There's been a social revolution you know!' That's what I'd wanted to say to them all, calmly, and with my face close to theirs, but of course never had done.

Patrick appeared, soundlessly at the foot of the stairs, his mouth in a daffodil-shaped trumpet as if he'd just been told the funniest joke of the year and he couldn't wait to pass it on. His face was looking particularly pink and smooth as if since our last encounter it had undergone one of its dermal renewals. He was wearing his usual navy blazer, grey worsteds, and horizontally striped tie, and looked as if he'd been here all his life, whereas I – suddenly feeling overdressed in my suit – felt decidedly conspicuous.

'I'll take you on a little tour; then we'll have a pre-lunch drink.' He said it as if his aim was to lure me into investing in, or buying something. He was evidently confident that he was about to give me an experience I had never had before, and in a way, he was right.

I was glad to get out of the entrance lobby and away from the misery of porter and registrar. As I followed Patrick across shoe-clicking marble onto noiseless carpet I could smell a concoction of wood, silver polish, and well-worn soft furnishings with no more than a drizzle of Jeyes Fluid.

He was a few feet ahead of me, and as we passed from

dark low lobbies into a towering space which was blindingly lit from above by a huge glazed roof he broke into a rhythmic skip which ended with a stamping-like dance on the marble floor. He resembled a little girl pretending to ride a horse.

It was undoubtedly an impressive space; colonnaded, and more than double-height with its glass roof bulging skywards as if it might burst and shatter at any moment. It reminded me of pictures of the courtyards in northern Italian palazzos I'd seen in books, only this one was roofed over. It was a temple but minus its nude muscular heroes. Other than the odd distant tap of shoe on stone, and even more distant bump of closing doors, it was devoid of sound.

'We'll come back here and have our little drinks upstairs.' Everything seemed to be 'little' now; little drinks, little dance, little girl, 'a wee bitty'. He waved his hand indicating chairs and table partly visible through the curvaceous stone balustrade above. Everything seemed to have a slight yellow tinge to it; the paintwork on the plaster walls, the marble columns, the lighting – I couldn't tell which, or all, or whether it was just me beginning to feel slightly queasy.

It might have been no more than my frame of mind, but so far nobody seemed to have made the slightest effort to put me at my ease. It would have been easy to suggest that Patrick was merely enjoying showing off, but I had the distinct sense that something more complex was taking place.

He was establishing rules, setting up barriers, defining the space between the two of us. But even if there was space between us I had a curious feeling that I was not safe. As long as I remained within the range of his magnetic force he seemed to be willing me along; onto soft deep-carpeted floors, and through rooms of various sizes and proportions. We appeared to be travelling in a large circle – presumably around the central glazed atrium. One space we entered seemed to stretch the entire width of the building. There were armchairs and low tables, some in alcoves and placed in groups, but the majority appeared to be in pairs. The chairs had high backs and unusually deep 'ears' so that the heads of anybody sitting in them could not be seen unless they leaned forward. Several chairs were occupied and I could see pairs of grey or blue worsted-clad legs.

'You'll be catching sight of one or two people who may seem familiar.' Patrick assured me, nodding, coughing, and fixing me with his black pupils as if he were indulging in some clandestine language.

It was true; as we passed the seated pairs I had fleeting glimpses of faces from the world of politics, and I had the feeling that though many intense conversations may have been in progress, the voices I could actually hear were no more than a hushed murmur. Still labouring under the force of my prejudices I sensed an atmosphere of dishonourable decay, this was a place where people gathered to eat meals which would be almost certainly of little merit while discussing people they largely already knew. It was as if the whole room were held in perpetual conspiracy by citizens of the super subtle.

I followed Patrick back to the main lobby and up two flights of stairs, through the atrium and onward. He opened yet another oversized polished and panelled door.

'This is the library.' He said it as if it were the only one in existence in the world. 'There are seventy-five thousand books.' Like the atrium it was deserted and to my surprise, full of well-worn architectural and interior design clichés.

Who had copied who I wondered? Sometimes even the real thing could look bogus. We moved on to the dining room to which we would no doubt be shortly returning, and I was surprised to see those gold dining chairs – the ones you see everywhere that you can hire for events ranging from Bar Mitzvahs to Afghan weddings; I would have expected something more authentic on Pall Mall.

There were three waiters standing by the *maître d*'s table and I was straightaway sure I recognized one of them; a tall, moustachioed, and untrendy young man wearing white shirt and shiny black trousers.

We returned to the atrium and Patrick gestured towards two leather armchairs which stood either side of a low polished table, and close to one of the marble columns. As I pulled at my chair and squeaked my way into its deep-buttoned hide upholstery he saw me looking at the surface of the marble column.

'Scagliola!'

'Really?' At first, I'd thought he was calling the waiter.

'It's not marble.'

'Ah.'

'It's clay, wedged in such a way that it resembles marble.' He smiled, pursing his lips and holding me in his gaze, no doubt with a mixture of irritation that I had not known this fact, and benevolence that he was lifting me out of a state of ignorance. '... A great favourite of Robert Adam.' I'd heard of him so I smiled back and nodded.

The tall moustachioed untrendy waiter I'd recognized in the dining room drifted towards us. I'd remembered at last where I'd seen him before. He was obviously an industrious and versatile young man.

'What are you going to have, Pulse?' It was a challenge; I hadn't a clue except I was pretty sure that this time it would not be a pint of ESP.

'A dry sherry for me.' Patrick's words contained the inflection that the waiter should have known that.

'The same please.' I felt dull, not for choosing sherry but for showing lack of originality.

'Are there any women members here?' I was trying to imagine Lauren sitting here… in fact I was struggling to visualize myself as a member.

His chair gave a sudden squeak and he looked at me as if I'd questioned his integrity.

'We began admitting women three years ago.'

'I see…'

'*We,* were the first to do so.' He made it sound like the Garden of Eden and that the male members had – not without considerable reluctance – agreed to sacrifice the odd rib in order to create female members. 'I won't tell you which, because you can look them up but there are already some notable names.' His mouth formed the 'O' shape.

It was strange sitting there in the atrium, which after all was little more than an oversized hallway. Every room at each level was connected to it. It was a public area, a route, a passageway, a vomitorium, yet it was endowed with a unique and perhaps uncanny sense of privacy.

'I want you to tell me what you think of the gents' lavatory.' He said it in exactly the same tone as when talking about his wines, as if he personally had a hand not merely in their use, but in their creation. 'I shall be remaining in the dining room after lunch so won't be able to benefit from your opinion so if you wouldn't mind going now…'

The toilets were in the basement, two floors down and were to my eye an over-flamboyant and eccentric celebration of the actions of bladder and sphincter. It was the scale of everything that appalled me. The hand basins were the size of the bath in my flat, the WC cubicles, though containing only one fitting, were each large enough to accommodate user plus an audience of six. The urinals resembled the elaborate sepulchral monuments to be found in European cemeteries. Each fitting not only had its *pissoir* headstone, it had a giant overmantel like a baronial fireplace which had been moulded with cherubs and flowers. All had been cast in fireclay which over the years had acquired a finish like that of gorgonzola cheese.

In contrast to the abandoned atrium, the library, the semi-deserted lounges and dining room, the lavatory seemed to be a centre of activity. Its heavy panelled cubicle doors bumped with regularity, conversation hummed, and laughter rebounded off the terrazzo and porcelain. Though the room was subterranean, its creator had achieved the effect of warm daylight coming from the ceiling. Bald heads shone, white hair glowed. Every few seconds came the hiss of tap water and the gentle thud of a hand towel being discarded into an open-topped polished wooden bin.

The walls were furnished entirely with mirror and divided into human-sized sections by way of dark mahogany panelling. The surface of the mirror had become patinated as its precious silver layer trapped behind glass had undergone the gradual process of disintegration. The result of frequent exposure to steam, and to the breath of men, of whom all – almost without exception – had not drawn breath for many years.

'… Quite remarkable, Patrick!' I voiced my opinion as soon as I entered the atrium and was two tables distant from where he was sitting. His head was tilted backward and he eyed me as if through a set of imaginary cross hairs at the end of his nose. Of course, I should not have raised my voice in such sacred surroundings and I decided not to risk his further disapproval with any detail.

He was sitting there, right leg bent, grey stripy socked ankle resting on left worsted-clad knee; his right hand cupping the dome of his polished black brogue. Before I had chance to creak my way back into my armchair he rose, the grey worsteds flopping back onto the domes of his polished brogues.

I followed him back to the dining room where we appeared to have the undivided attention of the moustachioed untrendy waiter. In spite of the fact that he'd served me with half a gallon of ESP over the two sessions at the Stag and Rifle, he showed no sign of recognition.

'I'm going to have the Brussels paté.'

'… I think I'll have the Dover sole.'

'I think you'll find it too much as a starter.' He spoke the phrase as if he were finishing my sentence for me.

'All right I'll have the Brussels paté.'

There were no more than a dozen diners and it was already twenty past one. None of the dozen was female.

'It started as a Whig club.'

'Really?'

'… Civil servants – particularly Foreign Office, although some of them don't actually work in the Foreign Office building – you'll soon learn what that means… Now it's predominantly politicians.'

'Is Martinique a member?' I realized my faux pas straight away. As a UN employee neither he nor she would be telling people even if she was. He ignored it.

'I'm going to have rib of beef.'

'I think I'll have sea bass.'

I could see the wine waiter approaching – not Moustachio, a smaller bald man; older. He was carrying two bottles, one in an ice bucket – both already opened. The bald man hovered directly above Patrick's glass, Patrick nodded, the man poured, the mulberry-hued liquid gurgled. There was no scrutiny of label, no tasting; he must have ordered, and tasted in the atrium while I'd been downstairs. The bald waiter filled my glass from the second bottle.

'It's Sauvignon Blanc, a Bordeaux; you'll like it.' It was an order, how had he known I would choose fish? There was something of decayed glamour, wine and witchery about it all.

'Your good health Patrick… Thank you!' I tried hard to make it sound sincere.

He fixed me with a sudden look of fury, a look I'd not seen before. He put his wine glass down, and with a great deal of care placed both hands on the white tablecloth, outside the rectangle formed by the cutlery, so that his square fingers were in perfect alignment with the knives and forks. It was as if he were an actor waiting in the wings, inflating himself with the oxygen of the character and was going to soar above his audience. He tilted his head so that I could see the bony tumulus of his Adam's apple. Before he spoke he gave a strange smile.

'I know exactly how clever *I* am, Pulse.' The skin around his mouth adopted the dark fissured appearance of the anus of some unknown creature. 'What I'm trying to find out is how clever *you* are.'

I stared at him feeling helpless. He'd been working up to this.

'I'm a straightforward man,' he continued, 'I believe in being open with people; *open, honest*, and *transparent*.' He pronounced the last three words as if they were the closing phrase of a sanctified credo.

'... Of course!' I could hear a slight indignation in my voice.

'It's my expectation that you and I have that characteristic in common. Any working relationship is a form of partnership... as intense as any marriage,' his smile widened in an air of self-congratulation as if he had proved the first stage of a long and complex equation. 'Its survival depends entirely upon trust. Each party needs to trust the other a hundred per cent.'

He knew that I was feeling out of my depth because he'd spotted that my relationship with Denise was a casual one. There was no commitment, he knew it, and I knew it. He was in possession of a voice of authority, he the master, me the pupil, I couldn't dispute it.

The moustachioed waiter appeared and served the paté and toast.

'I get the feeling... sometimes – that you like to play your cards rather close to your chest.' His smile was still a knowing one, but it had changed into a different kind of knowing. He caught me by surprise.

'I wouldn't like to think that you were hiding anything from me...' He stared at me with his black pupils.

'... Because if I *did* think that, and I found that I was

correct, then I'd have you thrown out of the front door just like that! How do you like the Brussels paté?'

I did enjoy the paté and I ate in silence wondering what to say next. He helped me out, but it didn't feel like help.

'It's quiet today because of the vote in the House.' He said it as if he sensed that I was upset and was offering words of calm. If they were intended as such they weren't having that effect. I'd suspected that he was a rogue, but for the first time I felt that I was sitting opposite a man who possessed little or no empathy with other humans. Quite possibly he was a man whose emotions were not genuine, and in order to give himself human credentials he had to play-act, to fake, to indulge in the histrionic.

I'd decided which way I was going to vote. Just because I'd drawn a blank with the telephone number from Hood's noticeboard didn't mean to say I'd come to a dead end. There was another pathway to explore, it would have signposts and at least one of those signposts could well be hidden in the third drawer down in Patrick's desk – the locked one. When I had finished this nice lunch and while Patrick was with his undisclosed and mysterious colleague I would be searching the drawer.

EIGHTEEN

I sat on the tube as it wormed its way north from Leicester Square, trying to calm myself. The sanctimoniousness of the man! He'd no right to imply that I might be untrustworthy, to give me a moral lecture. There'd been no outright accusation, no allegation, but there was the implication that I had built a wall around myself – never mind the fact that *he* was a past-master at constructing his own ramparts – and that he was doing me a service by trying to breach it. Between now and when I got back to the office I needed to achieve perfect balance between anger and enterprise. It would be no good flying into a temper and rifling his drawer out of revenge.

As I stared mournfully in front of me I became aware that the woman sitting opposite me was dressed entirely in yellow. Yellow flared trousers and a kind of oilskin top and matching sou'wester. She was sitting primly holding on her lap a large Hessian bag boldly embroidered in a kaleidoscope of colours. Further down the tube car was a large bearded man, very drunk, and who was attempting to sit on everybody's knees. Travellers were using a patent technique of dealing with his advances by holding up their hands, palms outward. This had the effect of bouncing the bearded drunkard, either to the person opposite, or rolling him onto the person next door. The man seemed helpless, like a giant hairy skittle waiting to be struck by a bowl. When he reached me, I followed suit with the other passengers sending him reeling across to the lady in yellow who hadn't cottoned on to the technique. The man sat buried in her multi-coloured Hessian and yellow flared lap looking gratefully around him.

'Arl-in-yellooo,' his voice strangely gentle as he attempted to encircle her neck with his tweedy arm.

'Get off me you bastard.'

Several hands waved in her direction in an apology for assistance, but with a jolt of the train he was up and rolling on his way. Once again, I tried to focus on the problem in question.

When I'd calmed down I would have three choices; i) to take it that Patrick had shown sincere fatherly concern for his and my relationship, that I should be grateful for advice and learn from it, ii) that I should continue to harbour my suspicions of him but do nothing further at present, iii) to use the energy from my present anger to take my search for to the truth up to the next level. By the time I let myself in through the front door of the office I had chosen number three.

As soon as I opened the black-painted front door I could hear the slow tap tap chug of the golf ball typewriter coming from the butler's pantry.

'Hello, Lauren, how are you?' I probably sounded tense, perhaps even breathless.

'Behind, hmm.'

'Patrick says he's coming back later.' I said it as a half question – a tiny inflexion at the end of the sentence.

'He's back at four, yes.' It was exactly 3.00pm. I had one hour to do something which I calculated was going to take me no more than fifteen minutes.

'I've just got to check something before Patrick gets back.' I hoped my voice sounded casual. I was glad Lauren was 'behind', it probably meant that she wouldn't be moving from her seat for at least the next twenty minutes.

I'd worked out that once I'd got the apartment keys from the top drawer in Patrick's desk I could be in and out of his flat in three minutes. If I was going to complete this little project in fifteen minutes that gave me… another three minutes to return the knobbly key to the cabinet upstairs and that would give me nine minutes to find what I was looking for. If I overran it wouldn't matter… in principle anyway, but I didn't want Lauren getting suspicious – or catch me red-handed because it was far too early for explanations. I had no Plan B. All factors considered the chances of getting caught were low but I needed to concentrate on staying cool.

Because the day was mainly a non-work day I hadn't brought my attaché case, so I went straight up to Patrick's office, taking care to walk on the creaky floorboard. Just for the exercise I tried the third drawer down, it was locked. I opened the top drawer, removed the two apartment keys and at the same time taking off my Chelsea boots which I placed together in the knee and leg refuge under the giant walnut desk. In stocking feet I retraced my steps, this time avoiding the creaky board. I paused on the landing; the tap tap chug was coming from the butler's pantry below. I raced up the stone steps to the apartment door and once again paused and listened to the remote percussion coming from the butler's pantry. I inserted the Chubb and gently turned, it clicked almost noiselessly. I repeated the process with the Yale and there was that delicious tiny sucking noise as if I was removing the exquisitely fitting lid of a secret jewellery case. I inhaled the scent of vanilla and as I did so I suddenly felt my confidence running away like sand through an hourglass.

What I was doing was bold beyond reason. If I was caught dismissal was a certainty, but what would dismissal actually consist of? It would be something infinitely more complex than the word it conveyed. To the rest of the world I would be a loathsome snooper, an invader and someone completely in the wrong, Patrick would be seen as an honourable defender of his property. Of course, he wouldn't go to the police; he wouldn't need them to assure him of his rights. I would be the cornered cowering child persisting with my pitiful excuses. What would be of much greater value to him would be my confession accompanied perhaps by my breaking down in tears on his shoulder.

'What ever possessed you, Pulse, don't I pay you enough?' He would say, while possibly even giving my back a fatherly pat.

In the space that existed between us he would know what he had done, and he would know that... somehow, I knew. But *what* had he done? Any crime he had committed would be absolved by the fact that I'd broken his trust, that's what his monologue in the club had been all about. It had been a declaration of moral immunity. There was no turning back.

I sprinted up the stairs into the kitchen and across to the knife drawer... Removed the key for the steel wall cabinet and opened it, noticing as I did that the knobbly key for the desk was no longer hanging on the extreme right hook, it had swapped places with another key in the centre of the row. I pocketed the knobbly key, locked the steel cabinet and replaced its key in the knife drawer. My hands were shaking and heart belting so fast I needed a split second to calm myself. Yes, I'd done everything right, so I padded down the stairs, pulled the exquisitely fitting door of the flat closed behind me, locked the Chubb, and after a moment's pause pussy-footed back down to Patrick's office, remembering to avoid the creaky floorboard in the antechamber. At the last second before I entered I glanced through the crack between door and jamb in case Lauren was in there. No, I could hear the tap tap chug. I'd taken under three minutes so far.

I had to hold my left finger and thumb either side of the escutcheon to steady the knobbly key as I inserted it into the lock. It wouldn't turn, I started to panic… try the other way, yes! Of course, he'd said, early 17th century it was a feature of the cabinet workshops in that eastern part of France, they produced locks which opened right to left – 'sinister', he'd boasted.

I pulled the handle of the drawer. It ran smoothly, softly, and it kept running, I kept pulling and it wasn't until I had three feet of the drawer open that I could see its back. That was right, Patrick had said something about the desk having being designed to take rolled up maps… but the top drawer – the one which contained the apartment keys was shallow. This was going to take longer than fifteen minutes.

Inside the map drawer was an intricate mosaic of notepaper, envelopes, greetings cards, and notebooks which had been painstakingly stacked. I glanced at a few cards, written notes and picked up one of the notebooks. It was packed with handwritten names, addresses, telephone numbers; I would need to work faster, I would also need to work on a hunch rather than to a system. There was a set of notebooks from Oyez stationers, marbled covers and endpapers, six inches by four. They were different from everything else in the drawer and all different colours. They seemed to be full of handwritten jottings of a personal nature; '...*heat, light, Freia, my mother, La Gomera*' were words that caught my eye... I could feel myself being drawn in...

No, this was what I was looking for. A notebook, marbled cover – not unlike the texture of the porcelain in the toilets at Patrick's club. There were lists of telephone numbers – just numbers, nothing else. They were sitting there covering each page as if they were secret codes. I scanned them, turning pages. Each number had a symbol next to it, '*phi, chi, psi, omega*', he'd categorized them. There were only ten pages – fifteen lines on each, so no more than a hundred and fifty numbers.

When I saw it, the thrill was like jumping into cold water, it was surprise but somehow, I'd just known it would be there; 01-241-0167. It was in the *Omega* category.

As I closed the notebook I dropped it onto the floor as I heard a loud report from the hallway below. Someone was rapping on the front door. Held in a state of deep freeze I stood looking at the notebook by my right stockinged foot and listening. It was okay it was just a courier. I could hear Lauren's voice in the Hall – 'Could you put it down there please.'

'Nah probs dahlynn, just sahn 'ere...' I heard the front door close and began breathing again. But there was something else; the courier's voice had been replaced by another male voice. *Fuck*, it was Patrick!

'… Are those the Fired Earth samples, Lauren? Is Pulse around?'

'He's around somewhere.' *Somewhere*? She was covering for me.

I could hear the leather brogues tapping and squeaking over the stone floor. A pause as he would be peering into the main studio, and then the sound I was dreading. It was like a grim cleaner scraping and sweeping each stone step with a besom. He was coming, he was coming, he was coming and there was nothing I could do. I just had sufficient time to replace the notebook where I'd found it, push the drawer back into the depths of the walnut monster and lock it.

The logical thing to have done next would have been to bluff it out. To go forward and greet him, *'Hello, Patrick, I was just searching for those photos of GI Group you were looking at yesterday.'* But just as I had lost my sense of time, my logic also had evaporated. I had to avoid contact with him, at any cost, and the result of my instinct was to force me into an even more impossible situation. As I heard him pass through the outer lobby I ducked down behind the desk and crawled into the knee space where I had left my boots minutes earlier.

Squatting, I turned my body so I was facing outward. In front of me was Patrick's dock-leaf coloured swivel chair, and beyond that was the central lower part of the medieval wall tapestry. I could see the lion's tail, the bottom of the richly patterned lady's dress and in front of that squatting – just like me – was the monkey, his haunches bent, his paws like mine resting on the floor in front of him. There was silence as if Patrick was standing by the door to the room sensing, looking around him, and wondering where Pulse was.

The space I was occupying was restricted by the height of the desk; it was three feet wide and almost five feet deep – practically the footprint of a WC cubicle. I could smell wood polish, carpet, shoe leather and – quite possibly – a trace of dog shit. I heard a floorboard creak – not the one in the antechamber, there was another I knew about over by the right-hand window. So, he was there, looking outside… or perhaps not, perhaps he was staring at the desk, his highly-developed and sociopathic sixth sense telling him that there was something wrong, that he needed to take care. I began to experience an unexpected relative sense of safety.

Knee space was an inadequate description for my refuge. Crouching there with my back almost touching the front panel of the desk, I realized that if I extended my arm fully in front of me it would not touch the knee of a person sitting at the desk – even with the chair fully drawn up. If one was alone one could stretch, out or lie in the foetal position and enjoy some degree of comfort. Were this entire object to be transported to the underpass at Waterloo Station a homeless person could live within it in comparative luxury and enjoy almost unlimited storage for their miserable possessions.

I could hear, feel footsteps close to my right ear, see grey worsted trouser material, hear the squeak of the dock-leaf deep-buttoned leather as it was pulled, pushed, and an abrupt rush of air as the bulk of a human occupied the chair in front of me. My secret chamber was plunged into gloom yet I was able to make out the curve of human buttocks against leather, worsted cloth drawn taut, and there was a notion of the faint line of a silver trouser crease.

I was visited by the awful realization that not only had I tampered with his private belongings, I had now secreted myself within his personal space. If he thought he was alone – which I sincerely hoped he did – then supposing he indulged in behaviour that one would only in the knowledge that one was alone? What if he did something unseemly?

There was the gentle woodwind note of the top drawer being opened. There was a silence and I began to pray that he had not noticed that the apartment keys were missing. I was overtaken by another thought which was accompanied by a marked temperature change in my body. When I'd been examining the contents of the locked drawer I'd failed to take into consideration the exact nature of my surroundings. The desk sat in perfect alignment with the left-hand window of the room. Someone walking along the opposite side of the road would have been able to look up through the window and see me bending over the open drawer. Patrick often walked there, enjoying being under the trees. On more than one occasion I'd seen him stand – and perhaps with more than a little pride – look up at the house.

The left trousered leg stretched itself, and I involuntarily moved my head to the left so that my ear was resting against the vertical wood panel of the drawer pedestal. The polished wood was smooth against my cheek. What an irony that inches away from my ear was evidence… shit, not evidence, not yet, it was still only a clue, I needed more.

I became aware that my ear was somehow enclosed by the wood. There was a small recess. As the leg of the sitter withdrew itself I turned my head and was able to feel with my right hand. It was a handle, a recessed handle. There was a secret drawer concealed in the volume of space that lay behind the shallow top drawer. It was invisible, even to a person glancing into the knee space from the front of the desk.

Directly above my head I could hear soft thumps. Of course, there were letters, put there by Lauren for Patrick to sign. I could almost feel him reading the letters – and even though alone – ostentatiously signing them. 'The use of bastard forms', was one of his criticisms of people's handwriting, and as I squatted in trepidation below I derived a morsel of amusement from the fact that though many might well use bastard forms, the signature above was undoubtedly being formed by a bastard.

'These will all have to be done again!'

It was a bellow clearly meant to be audible from the butler's pantry below. The chair lurched backwards, the grey worsteds lengthened, flopped over the twin domes of the black brogues. I moved forward onto all fours and listened as the footsteps left the room, the creaking board in the antechamber creaked; tap tap chug, this time it was the sound of shoe leather on stone, descending.

I tumbled out of my hiding place, forced my body into a vertical position, and winced at the pain that only five minutes of squatting could inflict. I dodged back under the desk and snatched my boots, skipped through the anteroom circumventing the squeaky board, and bending down to hide the boots, this time behind the door. I could hear voices below, the bovine bellow, and the calm *tessitura* in response. I raced up the stairs to the apartment door; the male voice below was softer now. In went the Chubb, then the Yale. I breathed the vanilla – there was something different about it, tobacco. Once in the kitchen I slid open the knife drawer.

There were several knives lying on the work surface which I was sure hadn't been there twenty minutes ago. I unlocked the steel cupboard and hung up the key. I locked, replaced the key in the knife drawer and carefully slid it shut. As I did so I experienced a sensation as if someone was pouring a jug of iced water on top of my head. There was a voice in the flat.

It was coming from the sitting room and as I made my escape past the door I could hear a high-pitched whining sound, impossible to tell whether male or female, but as the words came through the door I knew who it was.

'Debrouillarde! Aguerrie aux moeurs de la rue,' then it continued in English, 'I don't want you to marry that man. There's something evil about him!'

I tore down the stairs out onto the stone landing, turned, did the Yale, then the Chubb and, taking the steps two at a time, I arrived at the door of the antechamber. God be praised the voices downstairs were still going! I retrieved my boots and raced to the stair head... Oh Christ the apartment keys! I hurled myself back through the antechamber again avoiding the creaky board, pulled open the top drawer of the desk and replaced them. I hadn't deserved such luck, the two voices on the ground floor were getting fainter; they were descending to the basement.

My boots back on my feet, back at ground level and endowed with a new confidence I tiptoed to the front door, opened it slowly like someone would if they were using a key from the outside – as if I had just returned from going out to buy a newspaper – then I slammed it and strode down to the basement smiling broadly, if a little zanily.

At the foot of the stairs I paused and looked through

the door into the samples library. Lauren was leaning over the large white table which was covered with discarded corrugated cardboard and brown paper. In the centre of the brownish debris were stacks of patterned tiles.

'Come and have a look at these new Fired Earth samples, Pulse.' As I came nearer I smiled into his eyes but it was impossible to tell from the black pupils whether the wolf knew that he had just made a kill, or not.

NINETEEN

When I caught sight of my mother through the studio window I wondered what she was doing. She was standing on the pavement waving and pointing towards the front door and looking 'put out' as she might say. She wasn't *really* upset, and when I opened the front door I soon grasped that she hadn't seen the bull's head bell, her knock on the door had been so slight and I'd been buried so deep in my thoughts I hadn't heard.

Evidently out of the parade of new friends she'd made on the bus journey was a woman whose son was a civil engineer in Kuwait.

'The Emir's palace, you wouldn't believe it… A hundred square miles of marble, imagine that!'

A tour of Lloyd Lewis Associates studio was going to be a let-down after that. She was hunching her shoulders as we stood in the cool gloom of the hallway. Wearing her 'azure cloud' summer coat from Debenhams I could tell she was feeling the cold inside the house. She tapped her feet.

'Bare stone?' The practice couldn't have been doing well if the boss couldn't afford carpets for a house as grand as this.

'Keep your coat on for now, Mum.' She followed me into the studio.

'Lovely,' she said. It was the size of the rooms, the fireplaces, and the tall windows with their wooden shutters which seemed to impress her.

'... So, you have to open and close them every evening and morning?' I demonstrated, it was six o'clock and time to close down anyway, Lauren had already gone home.

'It's just like it must have been a hundred years ago. I se-e-e, it's like a museum!' She said it as if she'd just solved the final *Daily Mail* crossword clue.

'Ahem!' There was a creak of leather brogue by the open studio door. He must have been in the basement while I'd been letting mum in at the front door.

'Patrick Lloyd Lewis!' *(Conservative)* he advanced towards Mum his hand aiming for hers. He took it, broad thumb pressing down on her fingers while his four-square digits played with their underside. He leaned forward, brought her hand to his 'O' shaped lips, and still holding her hand...

'I've heard *so* much about you.' He *hadn't* – unless he was referring to her knitting accomplishments... Mum's top lip puckered, then she broke into one of her giggles.

Mum's giggles were rare, in fact the only time I heard them was when I was a child, and her fourteen-stone sister would come to stay. The three of us would sit on the sofa – me trapped in the middle, the two of them giggling away. I also imagine that she'd done plenty of giggling when Dad had been courting her so it was with mixed emotions that I now heard her.

His lips were still nuzzling her fingers when he turned his face to me.

'You've been keeping her *very* close to your chest.' It was delivered in exactly the same tone as '*I've been having a few moments with my late wife,*' and '*you sometimes play your cards very close…*'

I noticed the pinkness of his ear and recalled the gentle brush from the back of Martinique's fingers along his shoulder during my interview. I laughed at his apparent self-contradiction. Mum laughed easily, less of a giggle this time.

As if he had suddenly become tired of small talk and was implying we should get down to business the 'O' shape of his lips distorted as if it were the fissured texture around the anus of some unknown creature.

'Come!' he bellowed.

We followed, out of the studio, Patrick, Mum, and me as vanguard – up four flights of stone steps. Patrick was dressed in navy blazer, grey worsteds, but his tie had undergone a change. Its stripes ran left to right instead of the usual right to left or the horizontal. I struggled to imagine some significance for this change in pattern and gave up.

'You have to be fit to live here!' I commented, lamely as he opened the apartment door. The aroma of vanilla was still there but was overlaid by something dark, animalistic, and there was still that hint of tobacco.

'Oooh, but I am.' Patrick's reply was succeeded by another giggle from Mum.

There seemed to be no one else in the flat, but after this afternoon's experience I decided that one could never quite be sure. Patrick stopped and turned towards us, blocking our progress further into the flat. Evidently our visit was to be confined to the sitting room and he gestured with his hand towards the open door.

'Sit anywhere you like.' He spoke as if it were intended as a challenge, moving as he did so inside the doorway where he stood watching while Mum and I hovered wondering where to sit.

Because that afternoon the door to the sitting room had been shut, and during my fleeting previous visit it had been open but only one foot, I was unfamiliar with the space. The room took up the full width of the house, but because a third of its ceiling sloped upward from just above the low windows it felt smaller than the *piano nobile* two floors below. From front to back, both side walls were lined with storage units – as was the space under the two windows, with a mixture of open shelves, and closed cupboards. The only free wall was on the inboard one behind where Patrick was standing. There was apparently no TV or hi-fi, and the focal point of the space was a large table made from some dark deeply figured wood which seemed to hover six inches above the thick apricot-hued carpet. There were no pictures on the walls.

Mum was drifting around the room looking as if she'd been coerced into playing an extravagant game of musical chairs. Her outstretched hand was moving backwards and forwards patting each seating option in turn.

Under the window was a four-seater sofa upholstered in a fabric not unlike Patrick's trousers. It was so enormous that removal men couldn't have brought it up the stairs and it must have been craned in through the roof when the apartment was being built. There were two matching chairs each large enough to accommodate two persons, but what was attracting Mum's attention were the three remaining seats; a Le Cobusier lounger in pale brown leather, a giant suede pouffe, and an Eames swivel armchair, rosewood upholstered in shiny black leather. The triple bus journey and the vision of the Emir's palace seemed to have endowed Mum with an even greater sense of adventure. She decided upon the Eames armchair.

But instead of placing a hand on either arm and gently lowering herself into it she attempted to kneel on the seat, grasping the headrest in the way that a small child might throw its arms round the neck of a rocking horse. As she transferred all twelve stone of her weight onto the seat it began to revolve – azure soft-touch fabric against leather and rosewood, slowly at first, but as she tried to turn over, faster and faster.

'Oh... oh... oh...!' there was more giggling. Patrick advanced and planted two masterful navy-blazered arms either side of her onto the arms of the chair, and the Eames, complete with occupant, stopped dead. Mum suddenly had the weary look of a bewildered elderly person being stretchered by an A&E team into an ambulance and I felt sorry for her.

'Perhaps the sofa!' thundered Patrick.

I helped Mum out of the Eames, took her coat and she perched on the sofa's edge, while I sat in one of the huge adjacent chairs.

'Oh, I like your wardrobe, Patrick!'

Against the inboard wall was the only piece of wall-standing furniture in the room. It was a double-fronted armoire, a crazy pastiche of *Rococo* and *Art Nouveau* and finished in a pale grey distressed lacquer.

'It's an arm-*oire*,' He said it as if he were teaching a three-year-old a new word. Mum blinked obediently. Patrick moved towards it and with a combination of the casual and ceremonial unique to him, he opened first one door then the other. I could see why there were no pictures, with both doors opened flat there was little wall space left.

Inside, the armoire had been custom-fitted with shelves in contrasting burgundy-coloured lacquer and contained most of the things associated with the preprandial and postprandial. Prominent were bottles for the construction of cocktails, an array of red wine bottles, and a legion of glassware.

'They're not allowed alcohol in Kuwait. What Darren does is he gets a friend of his who lives in Doncaster to send him all the ingredients – the hops and yeast and so on in the post, then he can make his own... *I* make my own wine you know.' At Mum's last piece of information Patrick's mouth formed itself into the daffodil trumpet shape.

'Well you won't have had this one before.'

Patrick advanced towards us with three medium-sized wine glasses which he placed ringingly on the low table. He returned to the armoire where he removed a dark glossy bottle which was standing on its own. I noticed that the cork had already been drawn. He sidled up to Mum, his left hand cradling the base of the bottle while his right performed *glissandi* upon its slender neck. Mum sat bolt upright watching the mulberry-hued liquid gurgle into the glass.

'Cheers, Patrick,' I offered rather dully. He was fixing my mother with his jet pupils, waiting.

'... Specific gravity about 21. More than average acidity and very high on tannin...'

Patrick's face had the look that it might have had if he'd just been told the joke about the Irishman who burnt his neck while trying to iron his shirt collars... As if he'd been the recipient of a piece of information so inappropriate as to be downright offensive.

'Well, at least you will be able to drink the whole glass because unlike some, this won't have any sediment in the bottom. *Lees* I believe *you people* call them.'

'That's true,' conceded Mum defiantly, 'but none of my wines contain sulphites, which this certainly does!' I was amazed and considerably alarmed at my mother's candour. Patrick's eyes had gone pitch black, and the skin round his mouth not only had the appearance of the anus of some unknown creature, it looked as if it was engaged in a desperate struggle to repulse a sudden attack of haemorrhoids.

Mum did finish her glass – practically in one, and in spite of its heavy tannins, high acidity, questionable specific gravity, and its abundance of sulphites she asked for, received, and downed a second one.

'Do you know London well?' Patrick had recomposed himself and was eying Mum.

'I know where they have the Gay Pride march and I've been to Flanagan's – oh and we went to *Midsummer Night's Dream* in Regent's Park in…'

'Nineteen seventy-two, Mum,' I added.

'*Really?*' Patrick sounded genuinely excited. 'I was there.' He said it as if he was talking about some event of world-shattering implications, as he might have done if he personally had witnessed Lee Harvey Oswald entering a Dallas Warehouse carrying a rifle. 'Wasn't Puck good?' For the first time ever he sounded sincere, amiable even.

'I cried.' Mum was gazing at Patrick, perhaps trying to visualize what he'd looked like twelve years previously, and whether the two of them might have exchanged glances in the crowd. She changed the subject as if she couldn't bear thinking about the possibilities.

'My husband was here during the war – just passing through and ready to go to France after D-Day. Saw a Messerschmitt in Hyde Park... crashed of course.'

By the time Mum and I rose to go, I had revised the plan for the rest of our evening and phoned from the downstairs studio for a taxi. The wait plus the hour's taxi ride back to W4 would give Mum ample opportunity to sober up and we could get a pizza there.

I got the cabbie to drop us on the High Road outside the police station which was directly opposite Pizza Express. We both got out and as I was paying the cabbie I could see Mum peering at the back of a large BMW parked nearby. Conspicuously displayed on the inside of its rear window was a *Grateful Dead* logo.

'That's just how I feel,' she said, her eyes still on the logo. The day was beginning to catch up with her.

We sat in the glazed roof extension at the back of the restaurant, there was music playing – popular, some old some new... Loud enough to enjoy but soft enough to talk over. Mum was full of Patrick – 'If I were twenty years younger...' She looked happy – the first time I'd seen her look like that since Dad died. She leaned close to me and said, 'You know love; you've fallen on your feet there.'

I too felt happy, happy that she felt happy, and in spite of the weirdness of the whole thing that was happening to me, happier than I'd ever done before. Anything felt possible.

The voice in a song coming from the tape deck was warning me that not only was I my mother's only son, but that I might also be a desperate one.

TWENTY

Summer was almost gone. London had that flyblown post-late-bank holiday appearance when private gardens looked more neglected than ever, and people I'd seen every day while sharing a tube carriage into work seemed to have disappeared. Others had filled their places, and travelling on the District and Northern Lines I rarely got a seat.

As I strap-hung trying to edge my way down the carriage each time the doors opened, I found that everybody seated always seemed to be reading or writing… mainstream newspapers, free newspapers, handwritten notes, non-fiction, and fiction – many were reading the same novel. Each day by the time I arrived at my station, I would take a regular count of how many copies of *Hotel du Lac* I'd seen being read. There seemed to be an epidemic.

I hadn't been away. Holidays were something you kept to a minimum, two weeks away from work could mean coming back and finding somebody else doing your job, doing it better. That had always been the fear in my previous office, and though the ethos – if you could call it that – of

Lloyd Lewis Associates was different, the need to be there was just as intense. This was an age that heralded the birth of the control freak – well, perhaps not birth but definitely its propagation. So far, I'd used contract people to help me, hired on a week's notice, fired on the same principle but I was particularly looking forward to today as Shem would be starting work with us.

The last three weeks had been quiet at the office. Patrick and Martinique had been in France, were scheduled to have returned last night, and I'd taken the decision – following my adventures here and in the North – to have a period of quiet introspection. There was little point in me trying to find out more about the Freia connection with Hood and, if I was honest with myself, the most recent incident had shaken me. I would wait and watch.

Lauren had been keeping an eye on the office, and the apartment above – I hadn't been up to Patrick's lair since the wine-tasting episode with my mother. It had been a happy time. Al would turn up once in a while to use the photocopier, and Laurie had been there quite a bit. I enjoyed his company with his frequent disparaging references to Patrick – or 'Monsieur le Pseud' as he referred to him. I'd seen nothing of the two girls, I was glad.

It was 0800hrs on Tuesday 4th September. As I walked from the tube station and approached the terrace, I could see in the road outside the office the orange and blue stripes on the flank of a Ford Granada with the almost discreet letters – POLICE. I could hear the slam, slam, of driver and passenger door. I watched it do a tremulous three-point turn, and it rushed past me as I continued along the pavement. There were two uniformed officers in the front seats.

'Nothing of value's been taken, just personal items of Martinique's jewellery, hmm.' Lauren's usual *tessitura* had been replaced with higher breathless frequency. 'There was no sign of a forced entry – even the rooflight was intact, yes.'

Everybody seemed to be at the house. Al was in the basement, the twins in the butler's pantry talking to Lauren. There'd been a family meeting and debrief at 0700hrs rounded off with the visit from *the grasshoppers* – as Mel Dickson would no doubt refer to them. The stench of well-hung pheasant had been replaced with the air of suspicion.

It was unlikely to be a family member, and what indeed would a baroness be wanting with small personal items of jewellery? It would appear therefore that eyes were on me. I knew where the keys were, I was an outsider, and I might be seen as having reasons to resent he who employed me.

'Laurie's been spending a lot of time here,' said Bea.

'He's been smoking cigs in the apartment,' said Jen.

'He's been here every day this summer,' said Lauren.

It seemed that perhaps after all I was not prime suspect.

When the angst of the robbery had subsided and the family had dispersed, I went upstairs to Patrick's office. He was still in his flat. I found Lauren on her hands and knees in the en-suite toilet. Bizarrely enough I hadn't even known of the toilet's existence – rather like the secret drawer in the walnut desk it was hidden away, only this time in that space on the first-floor landing at the top of the stairs.

The en suite was a windowless box and lit by artificial means. It was surprisingly spacious and I couldn't help thinking that it had been designed rather like the American presidential en suite in the Oval Office, which under certain presidencies had earned the reputation as acting as an extension of the boardroom table thus enabling its incumbents to continue pontificating while they enjoyed a presidential crap.

'We really must find a new cleaner,' wailed Lauren. It appeared that not only had the cleaner left visible a can of Mr Sheen, but the toilet roll supplier had delivered the wrong kind of toilet rolls.

'What are the "right" ones?' I'd never really studied them.

'They have to be white, hmm.'

'But those *are* white.' I pointed to the fat little bale protruding from the wall on its polished stainless rod.

'No, *pure* white. These have got *things* on them – see!' She held up a spare roll to illustrate her argument. I let out a half-guffaw at the thought of the mounting discomposure of Patrick as he was forced to wipe his arse on a seemingly endless frieze of mint-coloured acanthus leaves.

As I turned to go I noticed that the floor tiles had been laid on the diagonal. Perhaps a demonstration of Patrick's extravagance as there was more wastage when laying the tiles, but more strangely an acknowledgement of the Islamic way of doing things. Their textile art which implies that the world does not end where space is intersected by wall, or the edge of the cloth, or paper. It was a constant reminder of the infinity beyond. A meditation on the invisible.

It was 1100hrs when the three of us gathered in Patrick's office, Lauren, me and Shem. Shem had said very little since he'd arrived. There'd been sniffing, grimacing, and a fair amount of foot-stamping on the molasses-coloured boards. Lauren had shown him round and I'd suggested he take the drawing board opposite mine. That left the remaining two workstations either for contract people, or further permanent staff as the workload increased.

We were sitting round the large white desk. I was facing the window with Lauren opposite me. Shem was to Lauren's right which meant he would be next to Patrick when he joined us at the head of the table.

'I like your ring,' Shem suddenly seemed to come to life as he looked at Lauren's hand.

'It's from the Baltic.'

'I can see that.'

I felt a pang of jealousy.

It was raining, the church clock was striking somewhere in the distance, and as it reached its final stroke it made a duet with the rattle of a Chubb lock being released from on high within the house. I heard the apartment door being softly squeezed open, and almost immediately closed again. There was a sound which resembled that strange percussive effect one experiences in a concert hall when the final notes of a symphony die, and for a split second the air is filled with isolated applause as if the audience have lost count of the number of movements and aren't sure whether or not they should clap. Perhaps Patrick had had his brogues resoled.

Through the window I could see Mackerel sitting on the balcony in front of the decorative ironwork waiting to be let in, and again I wondered how she had got there. The 'applause' ceased, the floorboard in the antechamber creaked.

'Typical English weather!' The male voice snapped as if it was not suffering fools gladly.

'Oh Patrick... your arm! What happened?' Lauren sounded emotional.

I turned in my seat, Shem rose – his hand outstretched ready to greet Patrick who was dressed in navy blazer, grey worsteds, and tie with horizontal stripes. But there was something extraordinary. The right sleeve of the blazer was hanging empty at his side. Under the blazer, which was fastened at the waist with one silver button, was an enormous bulge. His right arm was in a sling of elegantly-pleated lint from neck to wrist.

'It's nothing!' He raised his left hand as if in benediction.

'But what happened?'

'Laurie did it.' He pronounced it *Lawrghrrrie* and sniffed through his flattened nose as the roar of '...*rghrrrie*' died on his pouting lips. He sat down in mystifying silence. Not only had there been a robbery but it appeared that an assault had taken place. The offence was no doubt in the process of being dealt with by the very two police who'd rushed past me in the Ford Granada.

'But he's only a boy!' cried Lauren.

Mackerel had her face a nudge away from the glass of the window. Her head looked like a rather damp striped medicine ball.

Patrick, it transpired, had challenged Laurie to an arm-wrestling match – 'all good-natured,' Patrick insisted, but it seemed things got out of hand. There'd been no question of an assault and the police had been called to deal only with the robbery.

'I won't shake your hand,' Patrick addressed the still standing Shem.

'... Left?' Shem persisted.

'That would be indeed sinister. Are you settling in?' He eyed Shem.

'Very well.'

'I gather you're Polish, I'm *very* pro Pole.'

'So, am I mate, but which Poles?' Patrick ignored the question.

'Have you lived here long?'

'Finsbury Park, man and boy.'

'I've got something *very* interesting *just* for you, a client you'll like.' He studied Shem with his dark pupils. I felt a pang of jealousy, of a different kind from two minutes earlier.

'Tell me, Shem, do you drive around London?'

'… In a bus, mate.'

'You're familiar with Arrival Airways.' It was rhetorical. Shem said he wasn't.

'People's Airline – "no frills" that *awful* phrase, but it's not "bucket and spade" – another *awful* phrase, it's long haul, Nigeria and it's particularly the Lagos flights that are the problem.'

It sounded interesting, but wasn't Shem supposed to be *my* assistant, why was Patrick giving him his own job above my head?

The rain had come on harder than ever, and Mackerel's face was pressed close to the glass, a tiny disc of condensation in front of her mouth.

'It's the hand baggage that's proving difficult. These people want to take "everything but the kitchen sink," – *another* awful phrase, and expect to cram it into the overhead lockers. They need a system to measure dimensions of the luggage – something that's clear to the public so when an item is too big it's seen to be fair to everybody, no arguments.

I want you to go down there this afternoon, meet the client, take a detailed brief, and do a survey.'

'Aren't you coming?'

'Oh, n-o-o-o, far too many people.'

'Can I take Lauren?'

'Certainly *not*!' I felt another surge of adrenalin.

'Right then, thanks Patrick... Early lunch?'

'... If you must.' Patrick's facial expression was one of someone offended but cornered. For some reason I was unable to fathom, he seemed to be incapable of indicating that this was insubordination. Shem seemed to be having a bewitching effect upon him. Again, I felt a pang of jealousy.

'Could we discuss GI Group?' I couldn't help it, my voice had a slight whining sound to it.

'Pulse, you really need to get a grip on that job, now!'

'Well I was thinking, if I could report back to you and brief Shem at the same time?' I wished I hadn't made a question out of it.

'Not *now.*' It was a bellow. Patrick rose, and the meeting was over.

I looked at Shem. There was a look of mischief about him I didn't like.

'As it's my first day...' Shem spoke the words like an actor hamming it up just a little. 'I thought it would be nice for the four of us to have a little bite together just down the road. There's a lovely old eel pie and mash café in the market. You'd love it Patrick, all black and white tiles. They do a beautiful eels and liquor.'

'Ye-e-e-s, well...' Patrick sounded almost coy.

'... Not your thing eh, Patrick? You never know whether you don't like a thing till you've actually tried it.'

'Falco's coming in an hour, Patrick.' Lauren shuffled the desk diary open in front of her.

'Saved by the bell eh, Patrick, maybe another time?'

Shem set off, Lauren withdrew to the butler's pantry and I went to my desk to work on GI Group, I could get a sandwich after they'd gone.

Moments later there was a loud report at the front door. Lauren answered it and there was the echoing of a male voice, the sound of kissing followed by a loud thump on the floor above and more of the staccato applause on the stone stair.

'Hey, hey!'

'Ho, ho!' There were sounds of slapping of hands and shoulders, the stamping of shoe leather on stone and Patrick accompanied by another man, who at first sight appeared to be his double, barrelled through the door and into the main studio. The two of them were arm in arm – Falco's right in Patrick's left, while the bulge under Patrick's blazer bobbed helplessly up and down.

The man was the same height as Patrick, identical build, had a flat nose and a thick neck. He was wearing grey worsted trousers, white shirt open at the neck but no jacket. His face was deeply tanned, and his head of short white blond curls gave him the appearance of an oversized Renaissance cherub. The two of them cavorted up and down on the boarded floor as if they were performing in a comic Italian opera, though perhaps one involving a wounded soldier.

'Hey, hey hey!' He caught sight of me sitting by the window. 'What you do, what you do?' He bounded across and peered unseeing at the drawing I was working on. His face was close to my ear and could hear him panting softly.

'GI Group.'

'Heyyy! You betta gettit right, utherwize it the sack for you, huh?' The twinkle in his eye was insisting how funny he was, but his body language seethed with Sicilian malice. He turned and lumbered over to join his pal by the white laminate table. I noticed that his backside was conspicuously larger than Patrick's, perhaps the result of carbohydrate foundations laid by his mum, and so solid that even the stress of running a restaurant for most of his adult life had never undermined them. There was something of the giant baby about his movements and I wondered if he had been breastfed long after there had been a physical need for it.

In what seemed to be an uncharacteristic gesture of solidarity Patrick had – with a great deal of difficulty – removed his jacket, tie, and had undone the top button of his white shirt. He was standing by the table holding an A3 pad of white layout paper.

'Falco, I've had a few thoughts.' His voice sounded as if it was going to go into a coughing fit.

'Too much thinking, my friend, is bad for the head.'

Patrick laid out the A3 pad on the table, flipped open its cover with his left hand, the exposed fingers of his right struggling to unscrew the cap of the maroon Montblanc pen.

The blond curly-haired man bent over the table and studied the sketches, breathing heavily and speaking in a series of grunts while Patrick stood, feet together, his left hand touching his own left buttock each time the Sicilian spoke. It appeared that the restaurant design was quite advanced and I wondered why I was not asked to join the meeting.

'No, no, no!' grunted Falco as Patrick attempted to sketch with the Montblanc.

'Like this!' His fat fist snatched the pen and scratched away at the surface of the paper while Patrick's good hand patted his own left buttock. Falco saw me looking.

'Hey, hey hey! You betta get this one right utherwize I come and measure your feet for concrete shoes!'

Lauren appeared in the doorway.

'Your table's booked for 1.15, Patrick. You'll need to leave the restaurant at 3.30 at the latest for your 5.00 meeting.' The two men came out of their curious scrum, stamped out of the room and slammed the front door. Presumably Falco would be doing the driving.

TWENTY-ONE

I'd had a feeling it wouldn't be very long before I had my first confrontation with Shem. He'd returned from his assignment critical of Arrival Airways management, critical of me, and with the curious sixth sense he seemed to possess he'd got wind of Falco and the restaurant scheme.

When I came into the downstairs studio he was sitting at his drawing board, his legs stretched out in front of him.

'You've been having secret meetings!' His tone was accusatory, absurd, but I knew exactly what he was on about.

'It was all news to me as well.' Why did I sound so defensive? I *was* the office manager.

'You should know what's going on.'

'There's only one person here who knows what's going on.'

'So, you're blaming Patrick, it's all Patrick's fault is it?'

'I'm not *blaming* him I'm just saying that's the way things are run here, from the top.'

'So, you're just helpless! Why don't you ask him? Everything here should be more democratic.'

I knew I was lighting the blue touchpaper.

'Look, I'm the office manager, you work for me.' My tone was indignant and I could see him bristling with Polish umbrage.

'You asked me to come and work here. I could have accepted a better paid job elsewhere – somewhere less autocratic.' He stamped his foot, leapt to his feet and walked past me slamming the door as he went out into the hall. Christ! He was being difficult but I hadn't exactly helped the situation by trying to squash him.

I followed, turned the handle as if I expected the door to fall off its hinges after the treatment it had just received. I could hear the tap tap chug coming from the butler's pantry and tiptoed along the hall towards it. I paused at the top of the stairs to the basement and listened. Shem was downstairs talking to somebody, but it couldn't be Patrick, he was out. I glanced across at Lauren who raised her eyebrows with a 'you're on your own there' look.

Back in the studio I made a couple of phone calls to GI Group consultants and suppliers, there was no sign of Shem's return. I was about to venture downstairs on a peace mission when he noiselessly appeared in the doorway.

'Hockayy…' He spoke like someone attempting a crude imitation of a Latino patois before dropping into a powerful east European accent. '… Let's talk about Commoonist countrees!' He appeared transformed in some way. 'Lorraine says *you* were right!'

'Lorraine?'

'The Missus…' He was back into his north London patter. That's what he'd been up to – been on the phone for the last half hour. So, he wasn't as decisive a character as I'd first thought, but I had to admire him for asking for advice, and particularly his wife.

'Sorry about the outburst.'

'That's all right.'

'Polish people don't consider that they've got to know someone until they've had a flaming row with them.'

'I see.' He walked over and patted me on the back.

'We're all paranoid you see – because of Martial Law.' But from what Lauren had told me he was virtually a different species from the men of the Gdansk shipyards.

'Do you know what they call our local north London free newspaper?' I didn't.

'*The Informer*! You people don't know how lucky you are.' It was amazing how he could switch his identity from north London lad to politically conscientious expat.

I wanted to ask him about 'the gold' but that would do for another time.

'When Patrick gets back…' my voice had the tone as if I was about to come up with a really useful suggestion. '… Why don't the two of us go and ask him for a proper brief on Falco's restaurant?'

'Yeh, okay mate.'

It was a step forward but it still didn't solve my production problem on GI Group, I would still need another assistant.

As I crossed the hall I heard Lauren's low voice coming from the butler's pantry.

'…Fancy a drink later?'

'Yes, okay.'

TWENTY-TWO

'It must be half-time.'

'What?' I couldn't think what Lauren was talking about.

'Arsenal versus Newcastle at home, that's their important meeting, hmm.'

'Ha, ha, of course.' I pictured the two stocky, white-shirted, grey-trousered men in the VIP stand, alternately whooping, hugging, and comforting one another... One of them with his arm in a sling.

It was the first time we'd walked up to the Stag and Rifle when it hadn't just finished raining so there was none of the steaming foliage of our two previous visits. The air was distinctly cooler.

Just as we were crossing the road to the pub a red Porsche Targa 911 raced past us. I'd heard it coming, mistook the sports exhaust for a Kawasaki motorcycle. I'd never seen any cars on these narrow cobbled wyndes and it gave me an odd feeling. For the first time up here, I could smell that smell, putrid water... the canal smell.

'Where is everybody, they can't all be at the match?'

The pub was deserted except for two early-middle-aged men sitting in the saloon wearing floppy jackets and big flat caps. They reminded me of a pair of costermongers and seemed to be sitting in silence as if they were waiting for something. I had a strange feeling that something had happened, or was about to. Both men had empty glasses in front of them.

'Our usual seat, I suggest, yes.'

I got the feeling Lauren was urging me along, and away from the saloon bar. As we sat down on the banquette I could hear the double click of stiletto heels above my head and caught sight of two young Asian women disappearing through the door leading off the gallery. They were wearing school blazers and quite short identical plaid wool skirts.

'Shall I order?'

'I suggest you wait a moment or two, yes.'

There was something unusual in the air, something going on which I hadn't understood.

'You're getting the hang of Patrick I see?'

'Oh, yes…'

'He's got an amazing ability to keep his nerve, hmm… To watch, wait, and most important to listen – you wouldn't think it but he *does* listen. Lions lie in wait until the moment is ready to strike; bulls intimidate by rushing straight in. He knows exactly when to do which, yes.'

From where I was sitting I had a view straight through to the saloon and could see the polished wooden curve of the bar. It was just out of Lauren's sight line. A strange scene was being enacted.

'What you're always guaranteed with Patrick is originality. He never uses clichés, never copies, only reinterprets…'

One of the two costermongers had approached the bar and was standing there staring solemnly at the barman – who was the young untrendy moustachioed man with the white shirt and shiny black trousers. I could see that the costermonger had placed his empty glass on the bar top, upside down.

'Have you noticed how he'll never lead off in a conversation? That's what I mean about him listening, hmm. He always makes sure he gets your view first…'

The moustachioed young man lifted up the hatch of the bar counter, and I assumed he would be coming to take our order. Instead he strode up to the first costermonger, gripped the man's left shoulder with his left hand, and with his right twisted the man's arm behind his back and frogmarched him across the floor, through the front door and out into the street where I lost sight of the two of them.

'…Then he'll find something wrong with it. Even if – for the hell of it – *you* decide to play devil's advocate and come up with a view which isn't *really* your own, yes. He'll always contradict you…But beware of saying that you don't like something because even if you give him a well-argued reason for thinking so he'll find things that disadvantage you… you know the kind of thing – "Oh Pulse, I would never be so arrogant as to think that!" It leaves you feeling like you're the one who's been arrogant, makes you feel like you're the aggressor, and defiled in someway. He'll never settle on the simplicity of agreeing with somebody… To Patrick that would look like being weak.'

The barman had returned, dusting his hands. I must say I was impressed with the way he'd manhandled the costermonger, I wouldn't have expected that from someone so slim and youthful. He installed himself behind the bar just as the second costermonger appeared at the bar and slammed down *his* empty glass upside down. He was saying something – I could just hear it. He had a powerful Northern Irish accent.

'I want you to chockme oat, jusslike ya did to'im!'

'...He really is frightened of losing his virility, yes. Has he told you about the dreams he keeps having about all his teeth dropping out?'

'Er... no.' I was trying to concentrate on watching the development in the saloon bar. After a moment's stand-off between barman and costermonger I saw the bar top hatch rise for a second time and the moustachioed barman swung himself through the gap in the bar, this time with considerably more force, left hand to the coster's left shoulder, right hand twisting his arm behind his back and quick march out onto the pavement. The barman returned almost immediately, dusting his hands as he walked from the door.

'Was he dancing to Falco's tune?'

'Er... yes.'

'He gets sooo nervous when Falco's around, yes. Not that he's scared of losing the job; it's that Falco might think he's not being laddish enough. Patrick's like a schoolboy, so desperate to be liked, trying so hard, and that in the end he blows it and ends up getting bullied. Was he touching his bum? I mean Patrick – touching his own bum, not Falco's?'

'Er... yes.' I was straining to follow the small drama in the saloon bar. The second costermonger had reappeared in the front doorway.

'You're a marrked mon barrmon!' He disappeared before the barman could pursue him.

'Oh, Patrick's so clever. "Lauren, you're a star" he says, "you're a wonderful novelist but we're *designers*. All Mrs Umberachi needs to know is *what*, we can tell her *why* later." He never overtly reprimands, that would sully him, would turn him into what he might call an "old woman," yes…But it's still a lecture, subtly disguised. He's the master, you're the pupil. Don't you ever want to tell him to fuck off?'

'…Often.'

The second costermonger had reappeared in the front doorway.

'It's an IRA bomb for yew barrmon!'

'…He's got a disgust of anybody over the age of thirty-five who doesn't have children and he's as worried as hell that Al's gay – he isn't, he's quietly hetero, but that's not good enough for Patrick, he wants on stage showtime-shagging.'

'Hello, what can I get you?' It was the moustachioed barman.

'Hello! How are *you?*' I felt suddenly friendly towards him, partly impressed with his recent performance but more so from the coincidence of being served by him in the dining room at Patrick's club. I expected a warm response and perhaps I would learn something, but the man's gaze was deadpan, there was no acknowledgement of recognition whatsoever. It seemed that *down there* and *up here* were two separate worlds.

'Two ESP – on me.' Lauren was quick off the mark.

I'd noticed that the pub was starting to fill up and was conscious of a man walking past me and up the stairs. I caught his eye and he looked away abruptly. He seemed familiar – of course, it was one of the two men with big noses and black curly hair. He was the one who'd emerged from the gallery room looking as if he'd been about to burst into tears. He walked up the stairs, turned along the gallery, knocked at the door and disappeared inside.

'You know Patrick's children are a kind of revenge for his personality. Al's okay, Patrick's hang-ups about him are *his* fault, not Al's. No, it's the terrible twins that are the double nemesis. Have you ever noticed how he never refers to any of his children by name? He's got a psychological fear of Bea and Jen, almost as if they *were* one being, one *übermensch* which has acquired four arms, four legs, two heads, and two terrifyingly conflicting personalities intent on achieving greater ends. He's frightened of Freia's free spirit, the spirit that's locked away inside Bea – even though everybody thinks that Bea must be more like Patrick cos she looks more like him, yes.'

The barman returned with the ESP and Lauren paid. The man with the big nose and curly black hair emerged from the gallery room, walked briskly down the stairs. I got the feeling that he was making sure he did not catch my eye. A moment later another man carrying a Samsonite briefcase, and glancing at his watch walked past and jogged up the stairs so hastily that the briefcase banged into the wooden newel post as he turned the corner onto the gallery. He tapped lightly on the door and disappeared inside.

'…That's why he's so keen to impregnate Martinique. You've noticed how skilfully she parries his brickbats. He thinks that if she's carrying his child then he'll have more control over her, hmm. My God how he hated Freia's free spirit; she gave him the three – no two – children but… Martinique will eventually leave him you realize… he's wasting her time.'

As I leant forward slightly I noticed that there was a fireplace on an internal wall facing the stairwell. It had a deep muscular oak surround and tall mirrored overmantle. On the mantelpiece was an oversized wooden cuckoo clock which I'd have sworn wasn't there before. I could see its reflection in the mirror and felt a small wave of nausea pass over me.

'…Laurie's the worry, yes.'

So far during the evening Lauren had been looking into her glass. For the first time she turned to look at me with her thousand-year-old eyes – the way she'd done when she'd said *you could make a difference!* '…Something happened… in France when they were all there – oh I know Laurie's been here a lot as well, but when he hasn't been here he's been there with Martinique and something happened. Laurie hit Patrick. Patrick implies that Laurie's got a violent streak, he's not violent he's emotional. The two characteristics may go together but they're not the same thing. An incoming male lion always kills the cubs of the previous male you know, hmm.'

She tapped her ring on the rim of her empty glass. Outwardly its amber reflected the crinkly glass light fitting behind her head. Inwardly lurked its shady prisoner, its legs and antennae held fast, just as they had been without change for millions of years.

Almost immediately the moustachioed barman appeared and took our new orders. I looked up as the door to the gallery opened and straightway closed again. The man with the briefcase came smartly down, feet tapping, knees bouncing. Like the other man he seemed to deliberately avoid looking in my direction. The barman returned almost colliding with a bald man who seemed in a hurry to get up the stairs. The barman set down the two pints of ESP as I caught sight of the bald man knocking and disappearing through the gallery door. Lauren had her wallet ready.

'… No… my turn!'

'I have to go after this one.'

'You got the last one.'

'This *is* the last one.' The emphasis was on the penultimate word and the significance of her seemingly obscure remark about male lions suddenly hit me.

I felt an alarming chill run through my body as I realized what I must do next. And I would have to do it tomorrow, or if not tomorrow then the next day.

TWENTY-THREE

Y ou look familiar.

I'm on the train and looking at the head opposite me as it rests against the seat back. You're old so I can't think where our paths might have crossed... Couldn't be Rotary, Round Table, The Lyons, Freemasons, or the Civic Trust 'cause I wouldn't be seen dead within a mile of any of them... A regular Mr Lean and Slippered Pantaloon you are.

Next to you is a young man... Long head – enormous brow, and sticky-out ears. His neck is the same diameter as his head, making him look like a giant wine amphora – his lugs the handles to pick him up by and pour. Directly above him in the luggage rack is a very long turquoise nylon holdall, long enough to contain a human body. The young woman to my left is asleep – or pretending to be. A copy of *Flaubert's Parrot* lies closed on the table in front of her.

Across the aisle are two further women – fifty-ish. Blue stocking literary types; loud voices... Loud enough to compete with the disembodied voice of Karl. We know it's Karl because he said so before he began his painstaking list;

'a wide selection of teas, coffees, hot and cold drinks, cakes, sandwiches, baguettes…'

'I'm going to a funeral…' I didn't ask you where you're going but I can see why you're in a hurry to talk to me. It's to get away from the Human Amphora who is tilting dangerously in your direction and wants to pour out information you don't wish to receive. Funeral talk may be the great social dampener but you can't ignore it, you have to engage. To ignore the dead is akin to killing them again.

'Anybody close?'

'…My mother.'

'I'm sorry to hear that.'

'…Inevitable… *Tempus fugit*.' There's a pause, fatal as it happens because the Human Amphora has tilted beyond the critical angle of lean and his information comes spilling out.

'I'm going to a Queen fan club reunion in Stoke.' You gawp, I gawp; the Bluestockings gawp. 'It's fancy dress…' He gestures upward with index finger towards the turquoise holdall as if introducing us to an offstage character. '… My costume, I'm going as a smurf.' He smiles from lug to lug while I attempt to swing the pendulum back towards solemnity by asking you…

'Have you any siblings?'

'No.'

'So… you've been doing all the organization?'

'Yes, the worst thing is wondering whether anybody will turn up. The old girl fell out with just about everybody. I mean you can't exactly send invitations out for a funeral.'

'I like funerals. It's amazing how much you find out about people – the deceased I mean.' The Human Amphora attempts philosophical mode.

'Why didn't you bother to get to know them when they were alive?' I retort curtly.

'It was the Pastrami-on-Rye literary festival...' Bluestocking no. 1 is explaining to Bluestocking no. 2. 'Nearly all Sci-Fi... Not my thing having to press the vinyl with the Mind Wizards of Callisto – but we had a very nice little stall on the ground floor where it was quiet. Then would-you-believe in come a young couple dressed as pirates – man-and-a-woman, you know – terribly well done, bristling flintlocks, creaking leather, rattling doubloons that sort of thing, and they're both carrying live parrots – lovely creatures...'

'I've decided to go for curtains drawn.'

I haven't a clue what you're talking about... Oh yes, the funeral!

'...For the committal? You mean curtains open?'

'No, curtains closed. No one wants to see the coffin trundling through the doors to the furnace, do they?'

'They don't do it straight away you know...' You look so worried. '...And the smoke you see coming out of the chimney isn't necessary *your* loved one. They stack them up – like planes ready to land.'

'Burning burning; quiz question. Your house is burning down. What three things do you save?' Talk of burning has got the Human Amphora agitated. '...Take your time, take your time, it's a tough one.'

'"No flowers," I said to the undertaker, donations to Alzheimer's.'

'Here's an even tougher one. You have a stroke – lose your power of speech. What three things would you choose to display by your bedside that would best describe your character to your carers?'

'The woman was carrying the male parrot – the smaller one, lovely black and white markings. The man had the female – twice the size of the male and you know what he was doing with it?' Bluestocking no. 2 shakes head. '… French kissing!'

'*"You've got the cutest ass…"* You have to admit that Freddie Mercury writes the greatest lyrics; pure emotion, just look at me; listen to the quiver in my voice.' The second item is true. The Human Amphora has become maudlin, wipes moisture from his cheeks with the back of his hand.

'Have you chosen the music?'

'*Jesu Joy of Man's Desire,* at the beginning and *What a Wonderful World* at the end. She loved Louis Armstrong.'

'Have you ever wondered why pirates are linked with parrots?' asks Bluestocking no. 2 as no. 1 stops to draw breath.

'Yes… Long John Silver of course and the Caribbean.'

'Wrong!'

'Wrong?' BS no.1 clearly isn't used to being challenged.

'Robert Louis Stevenson wasn't just inventive. He was a humourist, and he liked wordplay. Pirate and parrot are almost the same word – particularly if you're from the West Country… "poirot and porot", go on say it!'

'Don't be ridiculous!'

'Go on, watch my lips; *pirate, parrot,* can't tell them apart at all.'

'RLS created one of the biggest literary myths. Take the wooden leg for start. Do you know how many people *actually* survived an amputation in the 18th century? …Near zero, prosthetics were virtually unknown. So, the whole culture of parrots, pirates, peg-legs, plunder, and Python has got nothing to do with history or life, it all came out of RLS's head. There aren't 'alf been some clever bastards.'

'What did you just say? …Oh, never mind!'

'Now then, now then, houzabout that then. Now then, now then, houzabout that then!'

It's Karl with the trolley. The young woman next to me who's just woken up asks for a tea with milk. I look across to see if you're going to have anything but you've gone.

TWENTY-FOUR

This time I'd taken the precaution of booking a hire car. That would give me full control over the ten-minute drive from the railway station to Brazzers... and back of course. The 'and back' was an ominous point for consideration.

What I was doing was probably seven parts mad and one part sane. Lauren's message was unequivocal; Laurie *could* be in danger, Patrick *might* be seen as a threat to him. But the two pieces of evidence I had to that effect could turn out to be no more than bizarre coincidence. If the link was genuinely sinister then I needed to establish a pattern.

My *must have* was further names, and more Dalston type telephone numbers. If Patrick was responsible for the death of Freia and her boyfriend, had used the services of a professional, and if he were thinking of repeating the process it would be logical to use a similar – if not the same – source. It was my duty to scour that noticeboard once and for all, and I almost felt that I was somehow being willed by Lauren. '*You could make a difference.*'

I got off the train and walked along the platform. As

I crossed the Station concourse the words of an Echo and the Bunnymen song coming from a coffee stall made me wonder whether I too was burning my bridges.

Why couldn't I let things be? I walked out of the station and made my way towards the hire car pick-up point. There was a future for me at Lloyd Lewis Associates, and there could be a future for Lauren and me – together. I had to admit to myself that the things that were driving me forward were those which are beyond logic, beyond intellect. The dream and the subsequent drip, drip, drip of the ephemera of *déjà vu*. My odd hallucinations on the train. Had I witnessed my past, my present, and was I going to foresee my own death? Because make no mistake, if things didn't go to plan I might very well not come back. I'd left a written statement in my flat, but that wouldn't save me.

I'd allowed a day's interval between the conversation with Lauren and my trip north to make preparations. I'd told Lauren and Patrick that I had a dentist's appointment in the morning. If things went okay I could be back in the office by two o'clock. I could have found an excuse to visit GI Group but I wanted Patrick – and Lauren – to remain ignorant of my presence in the north.

I walked over to the car hire stand, signed, and the young woman handed me the keys. With any luck, I would be back in half an hour and she would be thinking I was very strange indeed. It was a Rover 3500 – wasted on a slowcoach like me.

I drove down street after street of desperate pink terraces, past high walls that looked like prisons, through a wasteland of demolished buildings, past factories with castle-like towers, past cranes, past smoking fires. I could see the moors in the distance and I felt a sudden need to go to the lavatory.

I'd taken the decision to park the car some distance from Brazzers which would allow me to approach relatively anonymously. The street I chose was a hundred and fifty yards away and there were high red brick walls on either side which would afford me a certain amount of cover. But the problem was that there was nobody else on the street, I was the only figure for miles around.

The road sloped down, away from the club and I chose a spot to park twenty-five yards from a junction with a road which appeared to be exactly like this one, and with not a house in sight. I locked, looked around me, it was deserted. The land behind the walls a waste of dusty brick rubble where mills had been demolished and the sites awaited redevelopment. I walked slowly and carefully back up the hill towards the main road where I'd caught the bus on my last visit. The giant mill building with its menacing tower loured down on me. I was keeping close to the wall but feeling conspicuous. There would be no quick getaway. I prayed that it would not be necessary.

As I emerged from the road, which consisted of nothing but two high brick walls rising either side of me, I could see the bus stop to my left, where opposite stood the main door to the club with its beguiling crescent of pink neon. To my right, the road sloped upward towards the moor, the route the black Mercedes limousine had taken. Almost opposite me was the gap in the wall where the taxi driver had entered and where the black limo had appeared.

At last, I forced myself to leave the cover of the wall, sprinted across the road and, leaning against the wall of the club, peered into the gap. It was the now familiar scene of desolation; the pit head rusted wheel, the stained and scratched line of steel containers, and underfoot the black carpet of damp cinders. It was just gone 1100hrs, the sky had turned an industrial grey and I could hear crepitation of approaching thunder.

Somewhere, buried deep within the fortress-like mass towering above me was that coliseum of a dance floor, a stage upon which within a matter of hours thousands of the sons and daughters of the city would be rolling, trembling, and thrashing. As I passed through the breach in the wall and tiptoed over the muskeg of damp slag I too had a feeling that I was on a stage.

I stopped short. Three yards from the stone steps and, standing by the edge of the subterranean passage that led to the metal door, I could see the bulk of a ready mix concrete lorry. Its zeppelin-shaped superstructure seemed at home with the other rusted, scraped, and smashed artefacts. Its engine was idling. As I headed towards the stone steps leading down to the side entrance, a wave of rain propelled by a gust of wind hit me.

I jogged down the steps into the saliva-coloured brick trench which was already awash with black water. When I reached the open metal door I had to step over what appeared to be a thick snake which hung down the side of the trench, lay stretched across the stone floor, and disappeared inside the office. I was tempted to stamp my wet feet as I crossed the threshold but the last thing I wanted to do was to draw attention to myself. The industrial hum from the ready-mixer and the office door standing wide open gave the place the air of a building site.

I took the wad of fake mail out of my shoulder bag and waved it towards the ceiling.

'Post for Mr Hood, I'll put it on his desk.'

I noticed straight away that things were different. The girl on the desk wasn't the redhead; it was the blonde quiffed girl who'd been at the Railway Club. There was an atomic nudge of recognition from behind her impressively mascaraed eyes.

'Yoo can leave 'em thurr.' Her voice cut through the engine noise coming from the ready-mixer as she brushed the air in front of her with her beringed hand.

'I need to get them straight on his desk.' I shouted back and was amazed at the sound of my own authority.

'Yoo'l 'aftoo go *that* whey!' This time she formed her hand elegantly into a pointing finger which reminded me of one of those enamelled Victoriana wall signs. It was aimed at the other door from the office, the one that led to the toilets which I'd used on my first visit. I could see why the need for a diversion. The entire floor of the corridor leading to Hood's office had been excavated to a depth of four inches and was being filled with concrete, the tube depositing the contents of its tank in rhythmic belching noises like a boa constrictor attempting to vomit back its prey.

I dived across the office, through the door and into the corridor beyond. On the right was a sign which said Gents, and opposite, the Ladies. Should I pause to take a pee? This was the question. How long, two minutes? But supposing that Hood was on the premises, and that if I'd been two minutes earlier I'd have missed running into him? It could just as easily work the other way, and I blundered on to the end of the corridor where there was a half-panelled painted wood door with a stippled glass window. The glass twinkled as if lit from behind, and I tried to look through, but the scene beyond appeared no more than a fractured cubist jumble. I opened the door two inches, alert, ready to run.

As I swung the door open I found I was in what seemed to be a lost property office. The corridor continued, but on either side of me were double height rails containing a mix of garments; slacks, jackets, suits, uniforms, skiwear, and riding habits. The diversity of clients here seemed remarkable. There was a predominance of mackintoshes of various types. Everywhere was lit by fluorescent light and the pale macs hung there like rows of ghosts.

I made my way down the central aisle between the hanging garments and through a door into a much wider space – shallow to my right, but much deeper on my left. Here the rails were triple height and there were several gangways leading off crossways. More mackintoshes, for males and females; they were unused but possessed a curiously old-fashioned look to them. There were hundreds of them, gabardine, that's what this place had been – or still was – a gabardine factory and these were the finished products... A world of singeing, shearing, surface fibres, warp and weft, of fuzz and nap... An environment of tilling picks, right hand twist, warp-faced and warp yarn. An establishment which must have contained a hierarchy from owner, to manager, to sub manager, to weaver, to loom basher, to clerk, to cleaner, right down to the lowest of the low, the schloppers and schmearers.

Ahead of me was a pair of those grubby flexible plastic doors that you get in factories. I thought I might have missed a turning but there was no other path to follow. The doors led into a short blockwork-lined corridor at the end of which I could see a second pair of double doors, wooden ones with circular vision panels. The light behind them was bright and as I opened one of the doors the noise was deafening. It was a huge kitchen. Under my feet were red quarry tiles interrupted by islands of stainless steel. There were rows of shelving, racks, *bain maries,* bouillabaisse, gandy brassacers, deep mustard, clam chowder, frau hochstrasser, intolerance and fanti bocchananits.

Two white-coated, white hatted men were flash-grilling meat, one loading up the griddle, the other slamming it into the stainless-steel tower in front of him with a noise fit to waken the dead. Two others were standing by a copper cylinder which was suspended above a jet of flame. One man was stirring its contents with a long steel ladle, the other was about to stir, as if the contents of the vessel were so tiring to work that it needed two men doing it in relays.

'…Which way to Mr Hood's office?'

The stirring man jerked his left thumb backwards, and the standing man lunged with his ladle. It seemed that my way was to be through a door in the same wall through which I had come but ten yards to the left. I was in serious danger of entering into a state of panic. How would I find my way back? What happened on the other seven floors? Was there a basement?

It was a relief to get away from the noise. This time I was in a corridor which I thought I remembered; sticky lino floor, walls recently plastered, and the smell of mortar. It dawned on me that I had right-about-turned, and that the shape of the route I had travelled resembled a hairpin in plan. The next door confirmed it. It had been here when on my last visit I had seen the shadow of the cat and heard Hood's voice. Stretching in front of me was the corridor which led back to the Formica clad office and there on the left was the door leading to Hood's office.

But something was very different. The floor had been excavated to a depth of four inches and was awaiting the next batch of ready-mix. The first section of concrete had now been poured and plywood shuttering had been fixed across the corridor just the other side of Hood's office. It seemed unlikely that there would be a further pouring today until the first had dried sufficiently to walk on.

I strode the remaining few yards to the door, stopped, listened – nothing. Even the hum of the ready-mix motor was silent. I tapped on the door, nothing… Squeezed the handle; it was dark inside – thank God! I switched on the light and stepped up the additional four inches and into the office while carefully closing the door behind me.

I became abruptly aware of how nervous and exhausted I was, and it was all I could do to stop myself sitting down. But I had work to do. I crossed to the noticeboard and – using my right hand as a guide – examined every scrap of paper, my eye moving from left to right.

As usual the noticeboard was covered in information; footballers, jazz musicians, wrestling fixtures, past and forthcoming; displays of karate, racing, nuclear war, the Moors Murderers, and private zoos. There was also a welter of handwritten personal information. It was going to take me some time and I was beginning to feel so anxious that I found myself working with both hands, one supporting the other. Every so often I paused, strained to listen. What I was searching for wasn't coming up.

I must have spent ten minutes tracing my fingers back and forth across the noticeboard. Nothing, I couldn't even see the one with the Freia information on it. I stood back trying to make sure that I hadn't missed anything. This whole journey had been a waste of time, and I was risking life and limb for nothing.

It was only when I half-closed my eyes that I noticed that where the Freia note had been there was an empty square of cork. Someone had removed it – yes there was the drawing pin, someone had ripped the note away and as I half-looked again I could see another gap in the patchwork of paper, and another drawing pin this time with a tiny scrap of pale blue paper adhering to it. It could have been anything but I was so hyped up I'd convinced myself it was what I'd been looking for.

Out of desperation I looked on the floor, on the desk, rummaged through the waste-paper basket – anywhere where the two Post-it notes might have fallen or been discarded. There were definitely two notes and both of them had been removed. This was the end of the road, and what an idiot I'd been to pursue it in the first place. I had no alternative but to get the hell out and forget everything.

My brain was so busy commiserating with itself that at first, I failed to hear the sound outside the door in the corridor. It was the mewing of a cat followed by the sound of feet, one foot leading – the other dragging behind. I felt a sudden chill to my torso, just where I imagined my spleen to be. I could feel the cold touch moving, past my duodenum, liver, and round to my kidneys. It travelled into my pelvic area, across my thighs, down through my calves until the flesh over my entire body was creeping. The mewing and the footsteps had stopped and I heard a distinct metallic click. The footsteps retreated.

Before I'd even reached the door and tried the handle I knew it wouldn't open because I'd remembered that, unlike the door at the Railway Club, this one had a keyhole, it was lockable. I was a prisoner.

The first thing I had to do was to control my breathing… Breath is what develops curiosity, kindness, and self-respect, and it was keeping in touch with my breath and the laws of gravity that was going to save me from having a panic attack. It was also quite possibly going to save me from interrogation, assault, torture, and death – or at least make the whole process easier to bear.

Before I'd even stepped away from the noticeboard I'd had an idea of how to escape, but I was in such a state of deep freeze I was terrified to even think it in case the door suddenly burst open.

The room I was standing in was 2.8 metres high, but I'd noted that the kitchen, the gabardine factory area, and the dance floor were all 4.5 metres high. That meant that between the false ceiling and the original Victorian vaulted ceiling was a void – a series of voids. Almost certainly these voids were interconnected – when the whole thing had been a mill, each floor would have been a vast open space interrupted only by cast-iron columns. Somehow, it should be possible to move freely through or above each space. At the edge of the building there could be a way to the outside.

I needed to act fast; i) there was the distinct possibility that whoever locked the door might return at any second, ii) I was quite possibly on the point of some kind of nervous collapse.

It was no good climbing up and standing on the desk. I would be able to remove a ceiling tile easily enough but I would not be able to pull myself up. I looked around – praying as I did so that I was not alerting the sixth sense of any individual who might be in the vicinity, and about to return.

There was a visitor's chair, ten cardboard boxes stacked against the wall next to the metal filing cabinet. But as I moved back towards the door I saw it, an aluminium step ladder. As I opened it and climbed I fought to dismiss from my mind that it had been left there deliberately, for me.

I balanced on the ladder. A ceiling tile popped up at the touch of my finger. It was sitting on the flange of a metal 'T' section and I could see that if I could just get up there that these steel struts would be my pathway.

Standing on the top platform of the ladder I was able to pull myself up by rocking my arms and legs. Once above the level of the false ceiling it was possible to move and keep a vertical position, but only if I bent my head and knees forward simultaneously. It was paramount that I kept to the metal flanges. A millimetre's deviation could end in me plunging back through the soft fibre of the ceiling tiles.

The next thing I needed to do was to pull the ladder up behind me and into the space. When my gaoler entered the room, they would no doubt expect to find me cringing pathetically, either behind the cabinet or under the desk, awaiting torture and death. Removing the ladder would at least cause them a moment's confusion when they found the room empty. But even lying across the metal framework I could not reach the ladder to pull it up after me. In the end, I managed to lasso it with the strap of my shoulder bag and pulled it up through the opening below me. With the step ladder laid horizontally across the ceiling and the tile replaced, I was still a prisoner but with a strange new kind of freedom to roam this powdery no-man's-land until I could find a way to break free from the building.

Having gathered my breath and thoughts, I decided that Hood would not return so soon. His method would be to abandon his prisoner for at least a couple of hours so that by the time he put the key into the lock the internee would be a gibbering wreck. He might possibly leave his victim there all night.

As my vision began to adjust I looked around me. I was squatting on the metal framework which held the ceiling tiles with the ladder lying next to me. I stared carefully at the ceiling tile which I had just replaced, but because I'd turned and shifted my position several times I was no longer able to visualize the layout of the room below me. Where was the door, the corridor? In which direction was the Formica office and the outside wall? I could see my hand in front of me but only as shape and movement and I realized that I had no idea which way to go. I attempted to lift the ceiling tile but couldn't. Each time I shifted my position I could smell brick dust, old mortar, metal that hadn't been oiled, an accumulation of unwanted debris. I groped with my right hand and held up something almost weightless close to my face; it was a flattened empty packet of twenty Embassy Tipped cigarettes.

I would need to start again. I was going to need to create my own map with starting point, landmarks, ground zero. I must establish areas of smell, texture, and temperature. My watch said ten past twelve, I would time myself. I decided that the position in which I'd placed the ladder would form a kind of compass, its top would be my imaginary north – of course I'd be wrong, but so long as it was relative, the system could start to work and my map would begin to take shape.

I swung my body round so it was aligned with the top of the ladder. I turned and began to move forward, a foot at a time, fanning the air in front of me. After six moves I could feel sheet metal below me perforated with tiny holes at regular intervals. I was squatting on top of a cable tray, it was like giant Meccano, and it would make sense for me to follow it. For one thing, it would take my body weight. But it carried with it a special new kind of hazard. Supposing there were uninsulated power cables? I would have to risk that. I also had a new advantage; somewhere there was a light source, I could now see where I was travelling but I was gripped by an overwhelming drowsiness and realized that I desperately needed to sleep. I'd been on the go since 0500hrs and the stress had taken its toll on my nervous system. Without further ado, I curled up on the cable tray and drifted into unconsciousness.

I peered at my watch. For some unearthly reason, it said four o'clock, I had slept for four hours. I had need to pee and in the new brighter light of my over-world I looked at the odd assortment of stuff littering the cable tray and surrounding area; a shirt box, a pair of protective goggles, what looked like an anorak, and a tangle of metal coat hangers. Outside the cable tray and resting on a powdering of unidentifiable fuzz was a two-pound jam jar – without label, and though dusty it seemed reasonably clean. Praying that it had not contained caustic soda I relieved myself into it and left it sitting on the tray like a giant medical sample awaiting the attentions of health visitor with litmus paper.

I could now see some considerable distance in all directions. The cable tray on which I perched was a small part of a much larger system criss-crossing a huge area. Above me was the low dark vault of the ceiling with its knobbly cast iron columns each casting its shadow and catching tiny silver threads of light.

The floor – for in my present predicament that's what it was – was more difficult to comprehend. It seemed to be at different levels, angles, there were unidentifiable dark jagged lumps which almost reached the ceiling. Some things I could begin to recognize; heating ducts, pipes, nodes, ferrules. Here and there were sumps of different widths, depths – everywhere I looked was debris of various sorts and sizes. Lying on top of a cast iron pipe was another cigarette packet, Capstan Full Strength. The archaeology of my surroundings was taking shape, and where there was original brickwork there would be evidence of rolling and pipe tobacco, ancient dermal deposits, hair follicles, the evaporated bodily fluids of those who had hauled, clanged, and bolted into position the cast iron columns. I needed to focus my mind on getting out.

I could see the aluminium ladder lying ten feet away and wondered why it was catching the light. Had someone switched the light on in the room below? I strained to hear human sound, but all I could hear was a distant hum of unidentified machine parts echoing through space. I decided to follow the cable tray towards the source of light.

Sometimes I crawled, at others I adopted an animalistic lope, my backside swaying in the air while using my hands as paws to pad my way forward over the metal. I was now some distance away from the ladder and as the light became brighter I could feel my mind preparing itself for freedom. It was dashed. The cable tray came to a halt, and in front of me I could see no more than a vertical screen of perforated metal. Below me the space fell away the full four and a half metres. Beyond the metal mesh was a steel spider's web of lights, gantries, and rigs. Lacelike non-structures, and patterns of light and shadow were slowly wheeling across the smooth gunmetal floor. There was silence except for the faint mewing of a cat and, though foreshortened by perspective, I recognized almost directly below me the familiar figure of a man.

TWENTY-FIVE

The only consolation in having glimpsed the frightening scene below me was that I now knew where I was. The centre of one of the two bars adjacent to the dance floor lined through exactly with the end of the cable tray – the way I'd just come. My fear-stimulated mind recalled that it was also the way that Dickson and I had entered the main auditorium on my first visit. All I had to do was to return to the place I'd started from and keep going. That would take me to the edge… the edge of the building, somewhere in the vicinity of the Formica office… But my watch said five o'clock, and it had taken me almost an hour to get here from the spot above Hood's office. There was nothing else for it, I turned my body around and began my painful lope back. I sincerely hoped that Stripy had not given my position away.

Since my sleep, my senses seemed to have become more intense. My smell and taste were in a state of anticipation, but everything seemed odourless and dead, and I was filled with a sudden desire to return to the smelly raucous world of life.

The features of the unknown territory beyond the ladder

seemed to belong to an age older than the twentieth century. There were elephantine cast iron boilers, a metallic tangle of pipes between which I had to crawl, and I was forced to make frequent detours. Sometimes the pipes were so close to the vault above me, or the false ceiling below that I feared I would get stuck. It was how I imagined potholing to be, only above instead of below ground. The only form of rescue would be starvation.

I became aware of a different kind of luminescence and I now knew why when I'd woken up that everything had seemed lighter. The storm had passed and I could see spokes of sunlight coming through a row of windows ahead. They were tall, wide, and subdivided into two-foot by one-foot panes of glass with steel frames. Each reached down to waist height above the floor far below me and reminded me of the windows in a Victorian school where it was possible to open the top section by pulling on a cord which activated a pivot. I found myself balancing, holding onto the metal window frames with my hands, while standing on the edge of what must have been the ceiling of the room hidden below me. Only the edge of it would take my weight.

I felt a modicum of relief as outside the windows I could see the familiar sight of the saliva-coloured glazed tiles, and my eye was just about level with the cinder-covered surface of that desolate yard. I yanked on the cord and the opening section of the window plunged to the horizontal. By bracing my right foot against the junction of wall and ceiling I was able to get my left leg through the first window. I could feel the coolness of a breeze as my trouser leg rode up to my knee. I pushed off with my right foot while listening to the sound of my own panting. I was now perched in mid-air, astride the window frame and trying to force my head sufficiently low to pass under the pivot. As I tipped my right leg I lost my balance, fell through the open window, and was left hanging fifteen feet above the stone path below me. I must have looked like the victim of a short-drop lynching. I reached through the open window and tugged the cord as if I were hauling in the rope of a boat. When the bulk of the cord was hanging outside the window I gave a final pull. The window snapped shut, and I abseiled the rest of the way, trying as I did so to place my feet on metal frame, not glass. As my feet hit the bottom sill the cord ran out and I jumped the final few feet landing in the trench like a badly performing discus thrower.

Without pausing for breath, I lumbered forward, up steps, across cinders, past scratched and stained steel containers, and through the gap in the wall where I stopped, dusted myself down and attempted in some pain, to walk nonchalantly across the road. Well done Pulse! You didn't get the information you wanted but you survived. I could almost hear my self-congratulatory tones. Now all I had to do was walk to the car and drive away.

I rounded the corner of the street where I'd left the car. I'd parked it facing downhill away from the club but on the 'wrong' side of the road so the passenger door was next to the pavement. Leaning against it was a human figure; tall, yellow check suit, cigarette ash-hued hair, gold pince-nez. It was no good, there was nowhere for me to go, and he'd seen me.

'Wotcheer, Puck!'

'Hello, Mel, fancy seeing you here.' I was trying to pat the grime from my trousers, hide the tear in my jacket sleeve.

My face must have looked like a coal miner coming off a shift. I drew level with him and stopped halfway between the wall and his lanky form. We stood eyeing one another; I didn't want to be the first to speak.

'Sorry, Puck, Hoody, don't like loose ends,' he said it deadpan looking me straight in the eye. There was nothing I could say, I was bracing myself.

Without taking his eye from mine his hand moved upward across his body towards his inside jacket pocket.

'Guess what I've got in my pocket.'

'I don't know, Mel,' my voice sounded amazingly steady, my heart was about to go into full panic attack. It was no good running. Stepping backwards wasn't an option, I would be a perfect target outlined against the brick wall, better to move closer to him. Surreptitiously I moved my left foot forward. He saw what I was doing and his hand completed the movement to his chest. I tensed myself. As I brought my right foot forward his hand reappeared and he held it towards me, palm downward and cupped as if it contained something.

He lifted his other hand and held it forward in an identical manner, so that he looked like a giant musterlander in the act of begging. Then he began moving both his hands, swapping their positions and jiggling them about as if he were a magician.

'Choose a hand, Puck.' His eyes still didn't leave mine… Sod it! I pointed to a hand and he turned it over.

Curled and fitting neatly against his palm was a yellow Post-it note. His eyes still didn't leave mine. He resumed his hand juggling.

'Go on, choose a hand, Puck.' I motioned towards his

other hand; over it went revealing a pale blue Post-it note. I could read both sets of names and telephone numbers upside down.

'As I've said, Mr Hood don't like loose ends, and what with you being a decent, dilettante, consecrating sort of genitalman I know that you'll make sure that these fall into the right hands.' He held the Post-its towards me; I unpeeled them from either palm and put them into my trouser pocket. There was a trace of a smile on his face.

'So long, Puck.' He moved away from the door and we swapped places, him in the middle of the pavement, me opening the car door and getting into the driver's seat. I slammed the door, wound the window down.

'Don't do anything I wouldn't.' I couldn't manage a reply.

I turned the ignition, put into drive. The road was wide enough for a U turn. I could see his hand in the air, and as I passed him it went to his brow quivering in mock salute. When I reached the main road, I could see him in my mirror still standing there, still saluting.

When I got to the junction I made a spur-of-the-moment decision. Instead of indicating left and driving back to the city I turned right and drove east towards the moors. I had sufficient fuel to get to the first service station on the M1. I would return the car tomorrow, the fine – or whatever, paled into insignificance compared to what had just taken place, or what I was likely to experience when I arrived back at Lloyd Lewis Associates.

TWENTY-SIX

The car radio – like in all hire cars – had been tuned to a local pop station. An adolescent-sounding voice was yodelling the question, what is love, and does anybody love anybody, anyway? I switched it off preferring the sound of my own thoughts even if they were troubled ones. It was 7.15pm and I was driving east, a low sun behind me. On my right was a trio of long lakes with dams, on my left moor towering above me, rocks, and the fleeting glimpse of what looked like a small boy on the horizon; vanished, lost, perhaps for ever.

A sense of open space usually accompanies a feeling of freedom, but in spite of the extraordinary events of the day I felt anything but free. Until this moment I'd been acting on my own. I'd been able to spell out my own terms to myself, clear, lucid, and realistic. I'd known I was never going to solve the whole puzzle, been aware of my limitations, but at least while I'd been doing it I'd been my own master. The moment Dickson handed me the evidence was the moment I'd lost my freedom, and in that instant, I'd become Hood's man. Now I was under instruction, and I felt like a double agent turned by an enemy. I was like the native of an invaded country who has been forced to collaborate with the invader, and in a way, I'd been taken prisoner. Run away, disobey, and you take the consequences.

I was thinking of Lauren, and Shem – but almost entirely about Lauren. Whatever the result of their enquiries, once I'd contacted the police we'd be out of a job… so why couldn't Lauren and I set up in business together – okay I didn't have any money, but she did… with her contacts and my experience it could work out.

As I parked at the first service station on the motorway it dawned on me not just how exhausted I was, or how hungry; but how insecure I felt. It had been the reason I'd hung onto the car. It was a base, an anchor, something I could return to. Getting out at the service station, slamming, locking and walking into the building was a wrench.

From a payphone, I telephoned the hire car service and left a message saying I'd drop it off in North London by midday tomorrow. I decided not to try the telephone number on the blue Post-it note with Laurie Fournier written against it. Directory enquiries told me that 01-222-4386 was a Willesden number. I visited the toilets and under the blinking scrutiny of ultraviolet light, and the humid rush of a shiny metal hand dryer I attempted to make myself look normal.

I ate cheeseburger, fries, drank coffee, and hated them; but I'd wanted something fast, something easy to chew and swallow. Two hours later at my next services stop I drank more coffee, purchased a spare ballpoint pen, notepaper and envelopes – the small personal size on which children and old folk write thank-you letters. I stopped once more, contemplated taking another sleep, but I was too keyed up for what was to come. When I drew up outside Lloyd Lewis Associates it was 0200hrs – perfect. I parked in one of the residents' parking bays, sod it! I would be away well before the traffic wardens were up.

I switched on the interior light, took out one of the envelopes and addressed it to myself at my flat in W4, adding a stamp which I already had in my bag. On the notepaper, I wrote a brief report updating the previous one I'd left in my flat – names and telephone numbers. I got out and closing as quietly as it's possible to with a car door, I walked under a gibbous moon to the post box at the end of the next street. I posted, and walked back finding myself several paces behind a fox which was doing that funny sideways walk that dogs sometimes do. I could tell by the way it glanced over its shoulder that it knew I was there. Then it stopped, waited until I was three paces away, glanced behind once more and shimmied between the railings into the shrubs. I could have sworn it was laughing.

My selenium activities completed and back at the car I took out the notepaper and wrote.

Dear Patrick

I'm sorry that you have once again declined my request to be made an associate director of Lloyd Lewis Associates. I regret giving you notice so soon after commencing employment here – it seems no more than five minutes since I made the same request when you interviewed me!

I've been recently approached by two colleagues who have just set up in practice and they have asked me to join them as associate director.

I wish you and your practice all the very best.
Kind Regards

The latter statement was *almost* true. The answer to the question about the directorship I'd decided would be a foregone conclusion. I sealed the envelope, put it in my inside jacket pocket, got out of the car, walked up to the front door of the house, and, as quietly as I could, let myself in.

I wished I'd got a coat or pullover. It was freezing, as if I'd just slid into the water of a canal – just at the point where it passes into a tunnel. I also felt the need of an electric torch, every movement I was making was by way of street lighting spilling through the hall fan light. In spite of the iciness of the interior I removed my boots, tiptoed into the ground floor studio, and going almost by sixth sense placed them under the large white-topped table. I moved onward and up the stone stairs, through the door of the antechamber – avoiding its creaky board – and entered Patrick's office.

For some reason, the shutters had been left open, and in the street lights the walnut desk loomed like some giant rectangular toad encrusted with amphibious grime. I stole round to its rear, squatting down – like the monkey in the tapestry just behind me – and peering into the knee space, as if I expected to see Patrick there on haunches, blazer draped around shoulders, knees drawn up to his chin, eye patch glowing palely and his arm in a sling.

What I was about to do was more daring than entering Hood's office had been, and I knew that if I was confronted, and that if Patrick had a firearm, then in a court of law he might be considered justified in shooting me dead. By the time he'd reported the incident and the emergency services had arrived, the two Post-it notes would have been removed from the body. Why didn't I just call the police now? That would be the sensible thing to do, but I felt as if I was in possession of a secret, some kind of obsessional jigsaw, I *had* to have the final piece at any cost, I was a crazy boy collector; I needed the full set.

Just for good measure I tried the third drawer down. It was locked, so I eased open the top drawer and removed the two apartment keys. Two questions were knocking away in my head; i) how sound a sleeper was Patrick? Did he lie there motionless all night like a student, or was he a tremulous insomniac? Given his age he could easily be up every hour emptying his bladder... But what about Martinique, would the faint click of Chubb waken her? Was I mad yet again risking injury or death?

Question ii) was Laurie. When had that Post-it note been written? If it was some time ago and the order had gone through, then he was a dead man walking... if he still *was* walking? How long did these things take? Identify target, shadow, establish habits; work out modus operandi; analysis, evaluation, synthesis... probably very like doing a design job only the client presentation would be more severe, the off-site date critical, and the handover had to be 100% fatal.

I tried to run stocking-footed up the stone stair – God I was stiff after my marathon crawl along the cable tray. I listened, nothing – no traffic noise to cover extraneous clicks and taps; not even the far off subterranean hint of a tube train, they were long closed down for the night. But my adventures of the day had made me defiant. It was as if the part of my brain which generated the emotion of fear had been in some way stratified, like garden seeds put into deep freeze or boiled to stimulate growth in spring.

Over went the Chubb, I squeezed the Yale... The jewellery-box-lid sound of the door seemed louder – like human sucking and kissing. I stepped inside and eased the door closed behind me conscious of a change in air pressure. The temperature must have been five degrees higher than out on the stone stairs. If the bedroom doors were open I was in trouble... but the master bedroom door was closed. I moved, pivoting from one foot to the other, my body like the fulcrum of a set of weighing scales. I could feel the twinge of my sciatic nerve, the aching of my calf tendons. I felt as if I was teetering on the unlikely boundary between athlete and old man.

I made it up the carpeted stairs,

'Eehrr, eehrr!' It wasn't sexual, it was sleep talking, and male. A burst of monologue which increased in its sonority, and abruptly ceased. Christ, supposing he woke himself up, or both of them. I eased open the knife drawer, took the cabinet key, inserted, turned, opened... Took the knobbly key, closed, locked, returned the cabinet key... out of the kitchen, down stairs, opened door onto stairs. There was a repeat of the monologue following by a burst of male coughing. If he was coughing, then he was awake – he had to be. But I was closing the door behind me, turning key, and away down, down into the cool silent night.

Back in Patrick's office I felt oddly calm. The worst was over, I was sure. With the long map drawer open I located the Oyez hardbacked notebook with its gorgonzola cover and found the page with the telephone numbers and... yes!

There it was 01-222-4386 *Omega*. All I had to do now was telephone the police, once it was in their hands everything would be all right. I decided that I would hang on to the knobbly key; there was no point in risking returning it to its place in the cabinet upstairs.

TWENTY-SEVEN

I t was 0645hrs and I appeared to have spent the remainder of the night sitting in one of the dried-blood-coloured leather armchairs in the ante room. I felt terrible. In the state of semi-slumber my thoughts had roamed one landscape after another, each of the terrains concealed sinister underworld figures who were pursuing me. I had found myself engaged in dialogue; negotiating, bargaining, arguing, always with me at a disadvantage, my free will running away like sand. I was being forced to believe them, and eventually coerced into accompanying them…

What woke me was the sound of someone letting themselves in at the front door downstairs. I knew who it would be. I sat resting my head against the dried-blood-coloured leather trying to put aside bad thoughts and gather good ones. The leather was dewy where I'd dribbled during my half sleep.

Through the window I could see the trees at the end of the neglected garden, at last returned to their diurnal three-dimensional state after spending the night as no more than flat dark shapes. I could hear the sound of the shutters being opened in the studio below... First the ones to the garden window; clang, bump, bump... then those overlooking the street. There was a hiatus and I guessed that the person had gone down to the basement where they would be switching on photocopier, filling kettle ready for coffee – the water jugs prepared in the tinkling fridge. I could hear the footsteps returning from below, the click, click becoming clonk, clonk, as feet carefully travelled from the stone of the basement steps onto the wood of the butler's pantry, then back out into the hall and up the stairs towards me. Not only was I virtually paralysed after my acrobatics of yesterday, unwashed and suffering from lack of sleep, I had failed to do something. I had not telephoned the police.

I'd tried – several times during the early hours and while staring at the dark flat shapes outside the window I'd lifted the receiver, but I just couldn't do it. It was the knowledge that as soon as I did, a shattering change would take place in my life. Even the thought that my delay might prove fatal to Laurie or become a threat to me hadn't roused me from my fear of change.

'Oh, it's you.'

Lauren was standing in the doorway wearing black skirt and a closely-fitting black turtleneck. Of course, I'd not been able to let her know I'd been delayed till after she would have gone home. I decided to say nothing. Maybe Laurie would be all right, the whole thing a crazy set of coincidences, maybe the three of us could just go on together as if nothing had happened. She had some typed letters in her hand.

Without saying anything she walked past me into Patrick's office, paused in the open doorway, looking round as if she were sensing that something wasn't as she'd left it last night. She disappeared from view. I thought I heard the woodwind note of the third drawer down, but I had to be mistaken. Moments later she returned minus the letters. She glided towards the dried blood armchair – the one next to the window – and sat on the edge of its seat folding her legs underneath her, in that curious way she'd done in the Stag and Rifle. The dark rings around her eyes seemed darker than ever, her cheeks hollower, and there was that sensation of fidgeting you get when there's no actual movement, just an unspoken repetitive rhythm under the skin; skin, skull, soul, skin, skull, soul…

'What you're born as – or into – doesn't always help get you through life.'

What was she talking about? I looked at her, tried that humourless smile. I should have known it was no good trying to humour her. She'd been working up to this all night, had realized I'd been up to something yesterday afternoon and was going to make a speech. *My* mind meanwhile was straining to engage with any coherent thought, hers seemed to be racing ahead, as if she knew exactly what I'd been doing. But she couldn't know what I was going to do next. I was conscious of the smell of the canal which I hadn't noticed during the night. It seemed to be rising through the house.

'I suppose so,' my voice was weak. What *was* she implying? Was she referring to herself? …The closet baroness? We'd never talked about backgrounds, and – given my sketchy knowledge of the upper classes, never mind the world of drug addiction – that wasn't surprising. But I'd spotted – and some considerable time ago – that *she* belonged to both of those worlds. The once ermine-clad, truffle and quail-fed body had degenerated, and the mind with it.

Whether she came from a long line of honourable shooters and jackers-up such as the sultans of smack, or whether her title was to be found in *Who's Who* of the descendants of brown ale who'd socially climbed their way to the breathless heights of crystal meth I didn't know. I'd never studied the addicts' aristocracy, *I'd* been fortunate in that the journey from '*amy*' to *ecstasy* had passed me by. Unlike the inhabitants of certain housing estates who had not only inherited shit, but had discovered that whatever they did, or however hard they tried, they would never be able to turn that shit into gold.

Actually, that wasn't a view I'd ever held – at least not until my experiences over the last month. My opinion had been that since Duffy, Donovan, Bailey and The Beatles, anybody in the UK… with the right attitude and a modicum of talent could get on in life. *Anybody!*

Since the day I'd climbed up the wall at the end of my parents' street – the street people referred to as a 'cult-o-sack' – I'd believed that with dedication, determination, and diligence a different and better life was obtainable for all. Lauren fixed me with her thousand-year-old eyes.

'Everything that happens in this world is due to chance and coincidence – within the general laws of relativity.' It was a sermon, like one of Patrick's but incongruously deeper. She'd read my thoughts.

'I saw you as being different… thought you'd bring something of depth to the office. You've been disappointingly superficial.'

I was trying to concentrate on my breathing. You've *been* disappointingly…? So, she *did* have some idea of what was coming. Hearing this was even worse than trying to crawl to an unknown position of safety along a metal cable tray, with a psychopath and a sociopath roaming about a few feet below you.

'There's no divine pattern you know,' she rambled. 'There're no hidden messages, no God in the trees. There's no "this is how it was meant to be", no "we were meant for one another", no "I've found what I was looking for". There is no "small voice telling us what's right", no "everything will come right in the end", no natural justice, no *deus ex machina*.

'People lie, they equivocate, they deny; and afterwards they return to the pink and fluffy kingdom of coupledom. They use their families as an excuse, a defence. They tell you that family life is "the only way to be". As if they knew. But they've never been on their own throughout their adult lives, so not only do they know nothing about other people, they haven't even found out who *they* are.

'They treat you as if as if you've rejected family life, as if you think you know better. Every Christmas you have to read their round robins, the inexhaustible parade of exam triumphs, the tediously written accounts of foreign holidays. Some people never find a partner. It's not their fault...'

The 'yes'es and 'hmm's which had abbreviated her speech were gone, her words were stream of consciousness – a watercourse of misery. '...It's not because they've chosen a different life – a more bohemian one; they just might be disabled, disfigured, be social wallflowers, or any one of a multitude of reasons which are no fault of their own. That's real life...

'People despise you because you're childless. Women are the worst, women despising women... They'll tell you that having children is the ultimate act of creation and if you're not part of it then you're not creative. Rubbish! They're no more than consumers and absorbers. There's nothing creative about having children even if they all turn out to be Picasso, it's a biological process, it happens. Creativity is searching for and finding what's unique and original about you and the world, not just doing what five billion other people do. "...*Begotten not created*", remember!' She was screaming, I was gawping.

I tried to move my leg, the black blood-red leather creaking as I did so.

'...But of course, you, Pulse my dear...' Her voice took on the deviant air of someone else's parody of a toffee-nosed gent. '...*You* will go on, living as you think fit, doing things by the book, doing what you believe is right, doing what others tell you, just as you were brought up to do; and you will die loving no one, and loved by no one.'

She took a deep breath as if her lungs were being filled through every pore of her skin.

'Chance and coincidence.' She said slowly. 'It's they who are the real miracle to which we owe our existence. It's they who we should be giving thanks to, and who we should rejoice in, not some mish-mash mismatch notion of a universal creator... And by the way, I can assure you that the earth *is* older than eight thousand years, I know, because I've fucking well been here all the time... Christ's death on the cross – my fault.' She gave a throaty laugh which seemed to come from the corners of the room.

What! She'd never once mentioned religion and with all her blethering I'd assumed she was an atheist. She saw me looking.

'Don't look so dumb, Pulse. "Our sins nailed him up there." It's symbolic. Everything Man is given he fucks up. Some people do it less well than others, some get paid more for doing it but it's all a balls-up. Life is one almighty balls-up!'

Chance and Coincidence, she spoke as if they were people, as if they were long-awaited guests at a party, and the embodiment of a perfect ideal – gods... The gilded ones. And she had said those three words so quietly, as if she were popping shut the lid on a casket of precious jewels and locking it for ever.

Outside the window I could see pale sun, could hear the *wa wa, wa wa, chir, chir* of a song thrush.

'Don't you ever consider what other people think about you?' She was calmer now, the question no less unnerving.

'Well, now I know, don't I? You think I'm shallow.' My voice petulant, I felt it.

'Not *me*, I mean other people.' She looked at me as if she were teacher, and I were her tiresome pupil. All I could think of was something which had been rambling through my mind since I was eighteen.

'If you want to know I'm haunted by those words of Arthur Rimbaud. His greatest fear was that others would see him as he saw *them*.'

'H – h – h,' her voice was a series of truncated hiccups.

'Well, Pulse, dahling...' She leaned across and placed her thumb and forefinger on my wrist – against my pulse, as if she was in the act of proving that I wasn't well. I noticed that she was no longer wearing the amber ring.

'...The prognosis is worse than you think because what they think of you is what you *are* and what you will be – no more, and probably a good deal less than *you* think you are. That is *all* you are, and all you ever will be.'

I couldn't take it in. I would memorize her words and store them for understanding later when I was feeling better.

'...So, you can forget your ambitions, your aspirations that folk will think of you as "a good fellow". You can set aside the pompous notion that your actions will be speaking louder than your words, and that you will be judged by what you did rather than by what you said...'

I suddenly realized I was terribly thirsty and I thought of that first day at my interview when she'd given me the glass of water.

'...That you "lived life to the full", that you "didn't suffer fools gladly" – that you "were strict but fair"; or that you were a man of principle, or any other of the wearisome parade of funeral clichés. You can discount all those hours which you might have spent in doing charitable works.'

The eyes hadn't blinked – still didn't blink as she ploughed on with her grim oration.

'Oh, I admit you can't control what others think, but do you really think that other people are interested in you? I mean *you*, what makes you *you*; the inner personality – as opposed to you the commodity, or you the earner, you the provider, the consumer, the member of the congregation, the ally, the sexual liaison, the status symbol... You, as opposed to *you* the fall guy, you the stooge.

'When they send you "the invite" they're not interested in *you*. They want someone to adorn their party, compliment them on their taste; they want someone to prettify their dinner table. They'll only ask you *your* view so they can tell you theirs.'

The eyes had still not blinked, the irises practically the same size as the pupils. '...And there's a payoff for them, they want to patronise you, pay for you, to show you how they live their lives. They're confident because they know you can't pay them back – oh I don't mean money, I mean because you're always outside, outside their bubble looking in. You're an extension of them, and what they want you to be, no more.'

'What about family and friends... they know you better than anybody?' I hoped I was throwing her a lifeline but my interruption was a stupid one and I realized it as soon as the words left my mouth.

'They're worse. They label you from birth, are obsessed with your genetic inheritance... and *spouses...* ' she spat out the old-fashioned word. 'They swear they want you to stay the same when in reality they plan to all but genetically engineer you, then curse you for not growing along with them.'

'...You're talking as if people have no personality, no free will, what about being true to yourself?' My voice was whining, but why should it? I might have been feeling like death warmed up but out of the two of us she was undoubtedly the *real* invalid.

'How many people do you know are prepared to get into the river, swim over, and find out what the vegetation is like on your side? Tell me that! Get out!'

I suddenly felt that I was a waste of space sitting there in the leather armchair and that she was telling me to go.

'Go on, ask the question; shout it across the cemeteries!'

Her voice had become so distorted that I wasn't sure whether she'd said *cemeteries* or *centuries*. Either way I felt a chill pass through my body as if someone far below had prised the lid off the inspection chamber, and the ancient subterranean stench was rising through the building. It was as though the incongruous display of emotion was coming from outside her body. To get out was what I knew I had to do.

From somewhere above our heads came a metallic click, followed by a gentle sucking noise as if the lid of an exquisite jewellery box were being removed. There was a slow tap, tap, tap, like the sound of a snare drum. Every other tap was accompanied by the squeak of brogue shoe leather.

I looked up as Patrick appeared in the doorway of the antechamber. He was dressed as I had always seen him dressed, but he wasn't looking at me, and he wasn't looking at Lauren. He turned and walked past without speaking, and with the curious air of a somnambulist he closed his office door behind him.

'What was that all about?' I feigned indignation.

'If you don't know that then you'll never know anything.' The words sounded like a stick of celery being snapped in two.

'I'm going to go in, ask him for my directorship, and if he won't give it me then I'm handing in my notice.'

Her mouth made a sound like an old kitchen tap being turned on. I patted the letter which lay in my inside pocket, struggled painfully out of the chair and knocked twice on the door. There was no reply. I could feel the thousand-year-old eyes on me as I opened the door and went in.

As I closed the door behind me the truth hit me. After Lauren's bizarre outburst there was no longer any doubt in my mind as to who had made the decision to have Freia killed. She'd known, felt used, felt like Patrick's stooge. Exhausted as I was it gave me a new feeling of confidence.

Patrick was sitting behind his desk, his blazer-clad arms in front of him and his hands clasped over his stomach. He looked like a friar but a rather shrivelled one. All his attempts at a commanding relationship with the walnut desk seemed to have come to nothing. Sitting there he reminded me of one of those creepy chess set pieces which consisted of miniature medieval ecclesiasticals. He looked as if he should be sitting on top of the mighty desk rather than behind it.

'…Morning Patrick!' I sounded nauseatingly perky.

'Good morning.' He said it in the way that a less original personality might have replied, *what's good about it?*

'I've been wanting to ask you again about the directorship. You said you'd think about…'

'I didn't. I *never* make employees directors.'

'Okayyy… In which case I've got something for you.' I walked round the desk so that I was standing between desk and window. As I pulled the envelope from my pocket I noticed that somehow it had acquired a diagonal crease. I handed it to him, leaning as I did so across the corner of the desk. He peered at me as if I was a tiny child who had innocently picked something unpleasant out of the gutter and was holding it up for his approval. I stayed standing, thought it was better that way.

His right hand reached for the stainless-steel David Mellor paperknife, inserted its point into the top of the envelope, and deftly slid it along its edge. He replaced the knife on the table and pulled the paper from the envelope with his wedge-shaped finger and thumb. There were two rectangles of paper. One remained between his fingers, the other floated down onto the desktop and I realized that in my haste I had put the folded edge of the single sheet of notepaper to the top of the envelope and that the paperknife had neatly sliced the sheet of paper in two. He picked up the fallen half from the tabletop, held them both in the air, staring stupefied at them like a conjurer who pretends his trick has failed before mesmerising his audience with the unexpected.

The daylight was hitting the letter in such a way that I could see in detail the surface texture of the cheap notepaper. There were a series of hieroglyphs embossed onto its surface. Marks made on the sheets of the pad below when I had sat in the car pressing the ball point pen in agitation while writing the brief report for the police. From where I was standing four feet from his eyes I could see, plain as anything FREIA LLOYD LEWIS… LAURIE FOURNIER.

Patrick put the two halves of the letter on the desk, turned to the right, leaned forward in the swivel chair and buried his face in his hands. He was in exactly the same pose as he had been the first time I'd seen him, with the rampant lion on the wall tapestry directly behind him looking as if it were about to swallow his salt-and-pepper-haired head. He turned towards me without moving his hands.

'I did it for you, Pulse.'

I must have looked at him as if he was demented. At first, I thought he meant conspiracy to murder, but he hadn't seen the hieroglyphs – or if he had, he was ignoring them. He meant the opportunity, the chance he'd given me to better myself in life. Okay it was histrionic but he seemed genuinely dismayed.

'I did it *all* for yoooou…' he repeated.

The 'oooou' of the 'you' seemed to undergo an unearthly *tonic* blend with another very different pitch of sound. It was the unmistakable wail of a siren. It stopped and was followed by the slamming of car doors coming from below the window – four slams.

I turned and looked through the long window. Below me and standing in the middle of the road were two black limousines, and further down the street to my right I could see the familiar orange and blue striped Ford Granada – parked diagonally, blocking the street.

In the front limo I could see a driver and directly behind him a passenger – both uniformed. The personnel in the rear car were sitting in similar arrangement, and I could just make out the driver in the Granada, also uniformed. There was a loud report from the front door accompanied by the sound of Tyrolean cow bells, and it occurred to me that in the whole two months I'd been here that was the first time any visitor had dared pull on the bull's head.

I hadn't called the police.

I crossed the room to the door and opened it to find Lauren standing in the antechamber facing me. She seemed to have undergone a transformation. She looked tall, elegant, commanding, and I was abruptly aware of something I had failed to notice before, a distinct swelling to her belly under the close-fitting jumper.

'Would you *mind* answering the door!' She spoke to me as if I were a servant. 'I'll go to him now, he needs me.'

Downstairs I opened the door to two bareheaded men in tight-fitting suits. A further two uniformed officers stood behind them, one male the other female and standing either side of the top step.

'Come in!' In spite of feeling bemused I said it as if I had added *'I've been expecting you.'* The first two men entered and I shut the door leaving the uniformed man and woman outside. I gestured to the first two to stand at the bottom of the stairs.

'If you wouldn't mind waiting there, Mr Lloyd Lewis will be down very shortly.' Feeling like a rather dishevelled butler I retraced my steps to the antechamber and sat in one of the dried-blood leather armchairs – this time choosing the one near the window. It would give me a better view when Patrick emerged.

After some moments, the door of the office opened wide and the two figures appeared, standing side by side. They passed me looking straight ahead, walking slowly and sedately as if they were members of a procession at a coronation. I noticed that they were holding hands.

TWENTY-EIGHT

The footsteps descended. There was an exchange of words, inaudible to me but in tone resembling the call and response of the Anglican creed of affirmation. It was silenced first by one slam of the front door, followed by four slams from the limousines. The hush which followed was broken only by the distant subterranean rumble of a tube train and the frantic *chip chip chip* of a blackbird racing past the window.

After a unit of time that I was unable to measure, I heard the sound of a key in the front door, the slam, footsteps mounting the stone stairs – rapid purposeful, and possibly two at a time.

'Hello, Pulse.' Laurie seemed to fill the door of the antechamber and I was glad. He said it as if the two of us were exchanging mutual condolences at a funeral but there was a smile on his face. '…Just going up to be with mum,' it was as if he'd said, '*it's going to be tough on her but it's for the best.*'

I sat there in a trance until I heard the front door again… Footsteps in the downstairs studio followed by movement in the hall, rattling down to the basement, kettle on, back up to studio. By the time I entered the downstairs room Shem was sitting at his drawing board.

'…Morning!'

'…Morning!'

'I've just resigned.'

'You, bastard!'

He put the same emphasis on both words, nodding his head in time, and as if he'd intended to follow with a lengthy diatribe, but it didn't come. I collected my few belongings; scale rule, set square, set of Rotring pens, clutch pencil, two notebooks; that was it – into shoulder bag and I was out of the studio door. I walked to the front door, opened it and suddenly realized I had forgotten to leave the knobbly key on Lauren's desk for her to find. I'd guessed that the police would release her later in the day. I also needed to take my office front door key off my key ring and leave that, so I closed the front door with me still standing inside.

'Good fucking riddance!' I heard Shem's voice coming from the studio.

I walked towards the butler's pantry glancing through the studio door as I went. Shem looked mildly surprised to see I was still there. Then I stopped, about turned, and climbed the stairs to Patrick's office.

I couldn't resist the thought of opening the locked drawer for the last time. There wouldn't be any harm. My fingerprints were over everything but of course they were, I'd worked here. The police would eventually want to interview me and then I would hand them the Post-it notes… Or would I?

They were going to have a field day. Who knew what

was in the secret drawer at the back of the desk? Perhaps there were layers of crimes stretching back into history. Maybe the police wouldn't be interested in me – perhaps I wouldn't have to do anything else... except wait and read the newspapers.

I walked through the antechamber, into Patrick's office, across to the desk... Felt for the key in my pocket... into the lock... right to left... the lovely soft woodwind sound as I pulled open the drawer. Everything was as I'd left it early that morning, except the Oyez gorgonzola marbled notebook. There was something inside it.

Holding it open at the page with the 01-222-4386 telephone number and encircling the '222' was a finger ring. It was silver with a large piece of glowing amber which contained the shape of an insect whose antennae and legs were outstretched, just as they were when it had been imprisoned millennia ago.

When at last I closed the front door behind me I found another uniformed male police officer standing on the front step. I nodded, he nodded; he seemed to have no objection to my leaving. This time the Granada had been parked neatly in line with all the other residents' cars.

I walked over to the hire car and found a parking ticket had been scrappily attached to the windscreen. I got in, drove. The drop-off place was only down the road, past the huge brick church, past the pub outside which Ruth Ellis shot her lover, left turn and there it was on the right. I pulled up on the hardstanding outside the large glass window and for a few moments I tried to go over things in my head.

Lauren had always known there'd been no alternative

other than for her to play second fiddle to Martinique. Getting rid of Freia was an act of jealousy and one which she'd already practically admitted to me in the Stag and Rifle that time. But it hadn't been *Lauren's* jealousy, Patrick's pride had no doubt been pricked by the chinless wonder Freia had taken up with.

Having Laurie killed was the line which Lauren had refused to cross, and that's the moment I'd been steered onto the scene by my prophetic dream. When I'd shown curiosity about Freia, Lauren had recognized that I was following the scent. Suspecting that Patrick's murder of Freia would be revealed, she'd laid a trail, part truth, part fiction – not to convince me otherwise, but in an attempt to use *me* to betray Patrick; to do what had become inevitable, and to save her from having to do it. But I'd failed to be her rat, her squealer, and in the end, she'd been forced to inform on the two of them. She'd used her underworld network well; after all, the gilded ones are all connected, in one way or another.

When I reported to the car hire office they charged me extra for late return, plus another sum of money for the parking ticket. As I handed them the key I looked at my own key ring. There was an unfamiliar key on it and it took me a second or two to realize that the key I'd left on Lauren's desk wasn't the key to the office front door; it was the key to my flat. I couldn't go back now. When I arrived at W4 I would simply have to climb up the gas pipe and enter my flat through the open kitchen window. It would be a doddle after my ordeal at Brazzers.

I wrote a cheque and left. They'd already got the car doors open and were servicing it for the next customer. Its radio was blaring, and a comfortingly adenoidal female voice was assuring me – in song, that if I fell, she would catch me, time after time. But it wasn't me who'd fallen, I hadn't climbed.

My dream and the glimpses of *déjà vu* had been correct after all. Yet in the gospel according to Lauren it had all been chance and coincidence. No, I couldn't believe that. It was *my* dream, meant for me alone and there *had* been a pattern. But instead of getting on with the job I'd allowed myself to be ensorcelled by it, become enslaved by the high masters, and now having had their sport they had discarded me.

I'd failed… Failed to take the opportunity to better myself – like the day I had climbed the wall at the end of my parents' street and looked over – '…*just houses, they're just houses,*' I'd said as if I hadn't wanted anything to do with them.

In my slow-witted way, I'd failed to read the rules of Patrick's game. I'd been given a chance and I'd flunked it. Patrick's offer had been for another person – another man, or woman – no, it was always going to be a man, but someone different, someone better.

'I gave Pulse the opportunity of his life, and what did he do? He flunked it. I asked him the question; "Pulse, what have all these successful designers got that you haven't? Nothing, you're as good as any of them but you have to fight for what you want. You have to fight" – and he didn't.' It was true, I had convinced myself that 'taking part' was more important than fighting.

'I was sure Pulse was going to bring something different to the office, something of substance, something deeper, but he didn't.' It was true, I had ignored substance for the sake of something that was as ephemeral as will-o-the-wisp.

I'd been wrong about Bailey and the Beatles as well; out with the old, in with the new – *the old road is rapidly ageing*; the rise of the youthful underdog with fresh ideas, merit succeeding over class? It was a view which was oversimplistic, a cliché – even sentimental, and an unworthy interpretation of the complexities of British society.

I'd misread Lauren, underestimated her. She'd been right, and she'd been one step ahead of me all the time. Martinique *would* leave Patrick; he *had* been wasting her time. I'd naively thought there'd been a future for Lauren and me, I *had* been shallow. Worst of all I'd been blind to the presence of Lauren's unconditional love for Patrick.

As I crossed the road another thought occurred to me. Everything in my head was merely *my* version of events. The biggest mistake I'd made was to assume that out there somewhere lay the truth. Not so. What worried me most was the thought that Lauren might have known everything, and that the two of them – from the moment I recognized Freia's photograph – had toyed with me and tried to draw me in to form a devious and lethal triad. They had played at being their own high masters. Fear of being caught would have been all part of the thrill. I knew that feeling only too well myself now.

The Bull, of course! One of Zeus's many disguises. Another guise; the torrent of gold descending and impregnating Danae as she lay in her brass-lined prison. That was myth, it wasn't truth, but somehow the casual application of the legend's peculiar romantic logic made me feel better.

Oh, I would wait all right. I would read the newspapers, but truth in fiction is so neat... Carefully and cosily organized within the perfect sphere of its own narrative, with its formulaic patterns, and that little twist at the end. In the great cosmos outside that sphere lies an undefined constellation of half-truths. I had taken this job with the intention of getting nearer to the truth, but I now knew and for certain that there is *no* fixed truth. Any legal case is as good as its solicitor, their research team, and the barrister who presents it. Lauren and Patrick would have the best. In the universe, there are the gods, and the rest.

As I left the traffic roaring up the hill behind me and walked into the tube station I thought of Mum. I would not tell her the truth, or even my miserable version of it. It would be the first time I had lied to her.

FINIS